Fire! Dale thought in a quick moment of sleep-dulled panic

Tansy. The half-formed thought dissolved in a fit of coughing as Dale lunged for the floor, instincts taking over. Tansy was down the hall. In danger. He yelled over the serpent's hiss of smoke and the lion's roar of fire beneath.

"Tansy, get back from the door, I'm coming in!" Dale shouted, hoping she could hear him. Hoping he wasn't too late. There was no response over the rush of dry, burning wood and the voice of the fire. He ducked below the waist-high smoke and gulped in a breath before testing the knob. Blazing air surrounded him, and he yanked open the door and bolted inside.

Through watering eyes and the eerie red radiance that bathed the entire house, he saw that the bed was empty, and his heart stuttered. Then he saw Tansy....

She was lying on the floor. Out cold...

Dear Harlequin Intrigue Reader,

It's the most wonderful time of the year! And we have six breathtaking books this month that will make the season even brighter....

THE LANDRY BROTHERS are back! We can't think of a better way to kick off our December lineup than with this long-anticipated new installment in Kelsey Roberts's popular series about seven rascally brothers, born and bred in Montana. In *Bedside Manner,* chaos rips through the town of Jasper when Dr. Chance Landry finds himself framed for murder...and targeted for love! Check back this April for the next title, *Chasing Secrets.* Also this month, watch for *Protector S.O.S.* by Susan Kearney. This HEROES INC. story spotlights an elite operative and his ex-lover who maneuver stormy waters—and a smoldering attraction—as they race to neutralize a dangerous hostage situation.

The adrenaline keeps on pumping with *Agent-in-Charge* by Leigh Riker, a fast-paced mystery. You'll be bewitched by this month's ECLIPSE selection—*Eden's Shadow* by veteran author Jenna Ryan. This tantalizing gothic unravels a shadowy mystery and casts a magical spell over an enamored duo. And the excitement doesn't stop there! Jessica Andersen returns to the lineup with her riveting new medical thriller, *Body Search,* about two hot-blooded doctors who are stranded together in a windswept coastal town and work around the clock to combat a deadly outbreak.

Finally this month, watch for *Secret Defender* by Debbi Rawlins—a provocative woman-in-jeopardy tale featuring an iron-willed hero who will stop at nothing to protect a headstrong heiress...even kidnap her for her own good.

Best wishes for a joyous holiday season from all of us at Harlequin Intrigue.

Sincerely,

Denise O'Sullivan
Senior Editor, Harlequin Intrigue

BODY SEARCH
JESSICA ANDERSEN

HARLEQUIN®

TORONTO • NEW YORK • LONDON
AMSTERDAM • PARIS • SYDNEY • HAMBURG
STOCKHOLM • ATHENS • TOKYO • MILAN • MADRID
PRAGUE • WARSAW • BUDAPEST • AUCKLAND

ISBN 0-373-22817-1

BODY SEARCH

This edition published by arrangement with Harlequin Books S.A.

® and TM are trademarks of the publisher. Trademarks indicated with ® are registered in the United States Patent and Trademark Office, the Canadian Trade Marks Office and in other countries.

www.eHarlequin.com

Printed in U.S.A.

ABOUT THE AUTHOR

Though she's tried out professions ranging from cleaning sea lion cages to cloning glaucoma genes, from patent law to training horses, Jessica is happiest when she's combining all these interests with her first love: writing romances. These days she's delighted to be writing full-time on a farm in rural Connecticut that she shares with a small menagerie and a hero named Brian. She hopes you'll visit her at www.JessicaAndersen.com for info on upcoming books, contests and to say "hi"!

Books by Jessica Andersen

HARLEQUIN INTRIGUE
734—DR. BODYGUARD
762—SECRET WITNESS
793—INTENSIVE CARE
817—BODY SEARCH

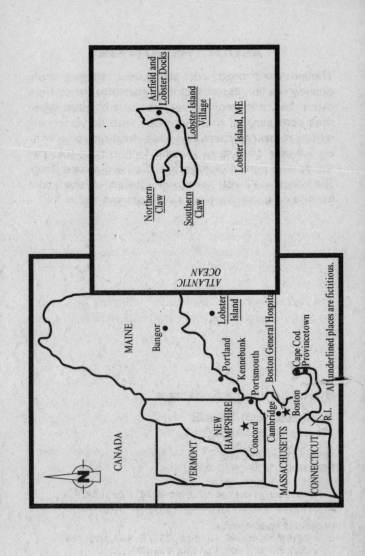

Airfield and Lobster Docks

Lobster Island Village

Lobster Island, ME

Northern Claw

Southern Claw

ATLANTIC OCEAN

MAINE

Bangor

Lobster Island

Portland

Kennebunk

Boston General Hospital

Cape Cod

Provincetown

All underlined places are fictitious.

Portsmouth

NEW HAMPSHIRE

Concord

Cambridge

Boston

R.I.

VERMONT

MASSACHUSETTS

CONNECTICUT

CANADA

N

CAST OF CHARACTERS

Dr. Tansy Whitmore—After this latest assignment, she plans to request a transfer away from the pain of working side by side with her ex-lover. If she lives that long.

Dr. Dale Metcalf—The outbreak specialist is a brooding loner. Will an assignment on the island of his birth break through his carefully tended walls before a deadly past catches up with him…and threatens the one woman he cares about?

Walter Churchill—Dale's father figure helped him escape the poor island and become a doctor after Dale's parents died at sea. He made Dale promise never to return. What will happen when that promise is broken?

Dr. Hazel Bronte—The island's dedicated doctor is overwhelmed by the deadly outbreak, which isn't playing by the rules.

Mickey Lowe—Dale's distant cousin and boyhood friend is the only one with the power to call him back to the island.

Nathaniel Roberts—The real-estate developer says he wants to help the islanders, but he may have a more deadly agenda.

Trask Metcalf—Dale's uncle drove him away fifteen years earlier. Is he looking to get rid of Dale again, this time permanently?

To Marley Gibson, for seeing this book through
from beginning to end. Thanks, friend.

Chapter One

People were dying on Lobster Island. Again.

Dale Metcalf read the brief message for the hundredth time and told himself he should walk away. Let the islanders save themselves—they certainly hadn't saved him fifteen years ago. They hadn't saved his parents. His aunt.

"Can I get you something else?" The heavily made-up waitress leaned over Dale, giving him a look down her shirt and a whiff of cheap perfume. She brushed her breast against his arm when she stood, leaving no doubt as to what *something else* could entail. Though the strippers were off duty, the Slippery Pole still reeked of sex and anonymity.

He lifted the nearly empty bottle. "Another beer, please."

Her pink-caked lips pursed and her tired eyes flashed, *stuck-up doctor thinks he's too good for the likes of me. Bastard.* She flounced off with a twitch of her too-generous hips, and Dale leaned back in his chair and closed his eyes. He folded the paper and tucked it into his pocket without looking, but the words pounded in his brain. Lobster Island. Death.

"Dr. Metcalf."

Dale jolted at the voice, then cursed when his boss, Zachary Cage, slid into the dark booth. "What the hell are you doing here?"

"Ripley said you were looking for me."

Hospitals were incestuously small by nature. Boston General had become even more so when Cage married Dr. Ripley Davis, who was best friends with Dale's ex. Awkward didn't even begin to cover it.

Dale frowned. He'd wanted to have this conversation at the hospital, wanted it official. "Yeah, I need to talk to you. But I didn't expect you to track me down in an off-hours titty bar."

"And I didn't expect to find *you* in one, knocking back cheap beer," Cage countered. "So what's the problem?"

Dale tilted the bottle to buy a moment. He wasn't much of a drinker, but the memories crowding his head deserved to be toasted with beer. The cheaper the better. He set the bottle down. "I need time off."

"No problem." Cage waved at the waitress and ordered an import. "Between Boston General and HFH, you've done the work of two average doctors. You deserve a vacation. Maybe it'll help you clear your head of…things."

Dale was tempted to let his boss think he needed distance from the breakup. But Cage was the local administrator for HFH—Hospitals for Humanity—

a group that sent doctors into unstable situations. War. Natural disasters. Outbreaks. He needed to know where Dale was going, and why.

At least some of the *why*. Nobody at Boston General needed to know all of it.

"I'll need HFH field equipment." Dale touched his pocket, where Mickey's message rested near his heart. Distant cousins, the boys had grown up together. Mick was the only one Dale had kept in touch with. The only one who had the power to call him back to that godforsaken place. "There's an outbreak of shellfish poisoning on a chunk of rock called Lobster Island. The Maine fisheries people shut the area down, but I'd like to investigate."

Cage's eyebrows lifted. "Why HFH?"

The subtext read, *why bother?* The group focused on major disasters and massive outbreaks. Not a few people sick with paralytic shellfish poisoning— PSP—and not when the locals already had the necessary quarantines in place.

But this was different. Resisting the urge to tug at his imported cotton shirt, Dale muttered, "I was born on the island."

Oddly enough, he wasn't struck by lightning. He glanced at his beer. It was his third. Maybe fourth. And it was the only way he'd been able to make himself say the words.

Cage raised his eyebrows. "Well, hell. I always thought—"

"Yeah, I know," Dale interrupted. That's what

everyone at Boston General thought, because that's what he'd wanted them to think. "I need a week, some field kits and lab support back at BoGen." He paused. "Please."

Cage studied him a moment, then nodded. "You can have all the equipment you need. But I don't let my team members go *Lone Ranger,* even on a quick island hop. You're bringing a partner."

Dale hid the wince, knowing Cage was bound by HFH policy. Nobody went into the field alone. Period. But he didn't want anyone else at Boston General to know about his past. Not even his usual HFH partner, though he trusted her as much as he trusted anyone.

Unfortunately, Dr. Tansy Whitmore wasn't an option. Not anymore. He scowled as the cheap beer soured in his stomach. That was the only reason he felt a twinge of pain that they'd gone from "let's just be friends," straight to "I hope you choke on your stethoscope and die, you miserable—"

"Slimy toad!"

Yeah, that was it. Dale looked up. The knot in his stomach grew tighter and he felt the familiar sizzle when he saw her striding through the disreputable bar without a sideways glance. Grown out from the short crop she'd given it during their last tropical assignment, her golden hair was caught mid-curl. It stuck out around her head like a nimbus of flame, matching the fire in her blue eyes. Her unpainted lips drew a tense line across her face, and energy crackled around her as she beat a path to Dale's table.

As always, the sight of Tansy was like a punch to his chest. But now, that first thrust of sexual awareness was tangled with other things. Anger. Disappointment.

Regret, though she'd never know it.

"Oh, hell," he muttered, rising to his feet more from self-preservation than manners.

Cage stood, as well. "Dr. Whitmore."

Hospital hierarchy didn't save Cage from Tansy's anger. She snapped, "Don't you 'Dr. Whitmore' me, Zachary Cage. You said you didn't know where he was." Without waiting for an answer, she turned on Dale and shook a piece of paper at him. "And *you!* What the hell is this?"

Her scent touched his nostrils, earthy and sensual like the woman herself. The dirty overhead light glinted off diamonds and gold at her wrist, neck and ears. Dale thought of the dull rock in his pocket, the only thing he'd kept from the island he'd once called home, and knew he'd been right to push her away before things got complicated between them. Like diamonds and ugly rocks, he and Tansy were too different to complement each other. Too different for a future, if he'd been looking for such a thing.

He glanced at the paper and forced detachment, though her anger raised an answering flare in his chest. She'd once called him cold, unemotional. Well, let her think that. Then maybe she'd go away and leave him to his beer. "It looks like my resignation," he observed, lifting one eyebrow. "I thought I left it on my desk, not yours."

"It's bull, that's what it is," she fired back. "You're the best outbreak specialist in HFH. How dare you quit?" The temper in her voice was familiar, but the glint of tears unsettled him. Voice lower, she continued, "If it's because you don't want to work with me anymore, I'll ask to be reassigned."

"Tansy—" he began, then stalled. He'd never known how to handle her emotions.

"Sit down, both of you," Cage ordered, waving them both to their seats. "Nobody's quitting or being reassigned. I've had enough of this."

Dale sat cautiously. Damn. He'd been writing his resignation when the message from Mickey arrived. In the flurry of memory that had driven him to the bar, he'd forgotten to hide the draft. Now there was no reason for Cage to loan him equipment or an assistant. Double damn.

Tansy passed the letter to Cage. "He's leaving. This was on his desk."

And what the hell was Tansy doing in his office, anyway? Since their breakup, he'd barely seen her.

Well, that wasn't entirely true. He'd watched her with her patients at Boston General, and he'd slipped into the back of her lectures and cursed himself for needing to see her. His only salvation was that she'd never noticed him.

Cage passed the paper to Dale and frowned. "Dr. Whitmore, I'm surprised at you. This is an invasion of Dr. Metcalf's privacy."

"I'm sorry," she said without a hint of remorse,

"but I'm not going to sit by and let him do something as stupid as this. HFH needs him, and—"

"And it's none of your business," Dale growled. "You have no right to try to get inside my head anymore."

She sucked in a breath. The quick hurt in her eyes made him feel like slime, though they'd had this conversation before. A hundred times, it seemed. Naturally open and giving, she'd wanted to know his every thought, his every feeling. But he had things he wanted to keep private. His emotions. His fears.

His past.

She rallied quickly. "We may not be in a relationship, but as far as HFH is concerned, we're still partners. That gives me some say."

"We're not partners anymore. I quit." Damn, he hadn't wanted it to come to this. But he couldn't keep Tansy in a relationship based on a lie, and he'd been surprised to discover that he didn't want to stay at Boston General without her.

"No, you're not quitting. I won't have it." She turned to Cage. "Reassign me to another HFH hospital and a different partner." Her voice was steady, but Dale saw through to the hurt beneath, and his chest ached.

"Shut up, both of you," Cage snapped, banging his half-empty bottle on the table. He waited until they subsided. "Okay. Here's the deal. I'm not accepting Metcalf's resignation or Tansy's request. But I am *fed up* with two of my best people ghosting around Boston General because they're letting personal problems interfere with their work." When they protested, he cut them off. "Just listen. Dale is leaving tomorrow to investigate a PSP outbreak off Maine. Tansy, you're going with him. Take the small plane, you can leave in the morning."

Tansy's startled, "But—" was drowned out by Dale's bellow of, "No way in hell!"

It was panic, pure and simple, that cranked his volume. He didn't want her anywhere near Lobster Island. He didn't want her to see where he'd come from. Who he was.

Diamonds and purple rocks didn't mix.

"You're going to the island together," Cage said in a steely, unforgiving tone, "or I'll fire both of you with prejudice."

Tansy gasped at the threat and Dale scowled. He was resigned to leaving HFH, but he couldn't get Tansy fired. The patients needed her. The group couldn't lose her. Damn.

Cage's expression softened. "Go to Lobster Island. Remember how to work together. You're the best team I've got, and it'd be a shame to let that go to waste."

"And if I still want to be reassigned after it's over?" she asked quietly, not looking at Dale.

"Then I'll reassign you." Cage sighed and stood. "But I hope it won't come to that. HFH needs you both. Together. Do we have a deal?"

His exit left a hollow gap in the conversation.

"Fine," Tansy said after a moment. She stared at one of the empty strippers' cages rather than at Dale. "E-mail me a list of equipment you want loaded on the plane. I'll meet you at the hangar tomorrow afternoon."

They'd had the same conversation a hundred times before, in a dozen different countries, but there was no sense of impending adventure now. There was only a sense of impending doom.

Tansy on Lobster Island. It was the last thing Dale wanted, but if he didn't agree, she could lose her job. And really, what did it matter if she found out about his past?

She already hated him.

On that thought, he drained the last of his beer and felt none of the alcohol's punch. "I don't want you with me."

She jerked her chin down. "Yeah, you've made that clear. Don't worry, the feeling is mutual. Too bad we don't get a vote."

She slipped from the booth and marched out on Cage's heels, leaving an aching hole in Dale's gut. "Damn." He pressed the empty beer bottle to the center of his forehead, wishing he'd chartered a plane and gone on his own. He hadn't been back to the island in fifteen years, since his parents were lost at sea and he'd run away from his Uncle Trask's brutal grief. He didn't want to go back now. And he certainly didn't want to bring Tansy with him.

Scowling, he reread Mickey's message. Six people were sick. Three had already died from respiratory failure, though the disease shouldn't be fatal. And although she was one of the best investigators in the business, Dale wished he could leave Tansy safe on the mainland.

Because people were dying on Lobster Island. Again.

HEADPHONES CLAMPED OVER her ears, Tansy slapped the throttle open and braced herself as the little prop plane surged down the runway, eager to be on its way. She'd gotten her pilot's license when she first joined HFH, nearly three years earlier. God, she loved to fly.

But not today. Today, the man brooding in the co-pilot's seat kept her from enjoying the sky. Arms folded across his broad chest, Dale made no move to touch the second set of controls. He merely sat there, sullen and angry.

Well, the hell with him. The breakup hadn't been her idea. She'd wanted to work on their relationship. He'd bailed.

She glanced at him out of the corner of her eye and tried to ignore the way the afternoon sunlight gilded his white-blond hair and accentuated his pale skin, which never tanned, even when they'd spent a month in the Serengeti. Long-legged and powerfully built, he had the hard body of a laborer and the graceful hands of a surgeon. His very presence filled the small cockpit, almost suffocating Tansy with the memories she'd tried so hard to avoid.

Both fair and blue-eyed, fit and wellborn, she and Dale resembled each other on the surface. But underneath, they were polar opposites, and those differences had been the problem. He wouldn't let her into his guarded, private corners, and she hadn't wanted to settle for less.

She glanced over again, and their eyes met. Heat flared in her midsection. After almost three months, she still woke up reaching for him, and despised herself for it. She was no better than her mother.

When they reached the shallow cruising altitude that would take them to a lobster-shaped speck off the Maine coast, she slid the headphones off one ear and broke the silence. "Want to tell me why we're investigating a tiny outbreak of PSP?"

Paralytic shellfish poisoning was a serious, though rarely fatal, condition that was usually handled on the local level. From what little Cage had told her, there was no reason for HFH intervention. But she knew Dale well enough to realize he wasn't going to volunteer any information. He was too committed to his bad mood.

After a long moment he sighed and uncrossed his arms. "It doesn't look like typical shellfish poisoning. The reactions are too severe, and there hasn't been a red tide in the area. Besides, the islanders fish for lobsters, not mollusks."

"And lobsters, being scavengers, don't usually absorb enough of the toxin to be a problem." Tansy nodded, glad he had at least answered her. Though it hurt to sit near him and know there was no hope for their relationship, she would be okay if she focused on the job. Always the job. Her work had gotten her through the last three months. It would get her through the next few days.

Besides, they usually got along fine when they were in the field. It was his behavior in Boston that had driven her crazy. When they were at home base, he withdrew, became unavailable. Toward the end, she'd wondered whether he had another woman in the city.

Know your man inside and out, and you'll never be surprised, baby. Her mother's words came to her across the years, along with the memory of sitting in the car while Eva Whitmore cruised their ritzy neighborhood in search of her husband's vehicle.

Feeling the familiar tightness in her stomach, Tansy clenched her teeth and concentrated on flying, as the sun sank towards twilight. She'd make it through this one last assignment with Dale, and then she'd leave. She couldn't stand seeing him every day. Not like this. Though in the end she'd been the one to walk away from their relationship, he had pushed her there.

He simply hadn't cared as much as she did.

"We're almost there." The voice was thick from the silence. The rough timbre heated the back of her neck with memory, and she stared harder out the cockpit window. The shadow of an island appeared, black against the gray sea. The granite claws arced around a central harbor at one end. The subtle curve of tail at the other end completed the illusion and created a second harbor.

She craned her neck to follow the rocky contours as she flew past and came around to face the northernmost claw. "Damn. It *does* look like a lobster."

"That's why they call it Lobster Island," Dale muttered as they began their descent.

Frustrated by his mood and his nearness, she snapped, "This trip wasn't my idea, you know."

"Wasn't mine either," he growled in return. "I tried to leave you home."

Tansy compressed her lips and concentrated on flying. Maybe she should've refused the assignment and risked her job. But part of her had wanted this one last trip with Dale. Away from Boston General, she knew she would see the man beneath the brittle upper-crust charm. The man she'd fallen for. In the field, Dale Metcalf was a bit loud and a bit rough. Exciting. Almost uncivilized. More at home in the slums of the small, hot country of Tehru than the Theater District of Boston.

But the moment they returned to the city, that man disappeared and was replaced by someone else. She didn't like the other Dale much, nor did she trust him. There was something…false about him in the city.

She darted a glance at the pale, perfect features of Boston General's most eligible bachelor. His square jaw was tight with tension, the lines beside his mouth deeper than she remembered. Though they were headed into the field, he had avoided his usual attire of bush pants and a cotton shirt. Instead, he wore a monogrammed shirt from England and lightweight wool trousers.

He was wearing his Boston clothes, Tansy realized. Not his field clothes. She felt a strange, unexpected stir of fear. Her mother had taught her that if she knew everything and understood everything, she'd never be out of control. That had made medicine a perfect career choice. Tansy understood illness, understood health. But as the little plane dropped through a scattering of clouds and shimmied in a slap of crosswind, she realized she didn't know everything about this assignment.

And she knew even less about the man sitting beside her.

Worried now, though for no good reason, she sideslipped the plane to lose altitude and radioed her approach to the Lobster Island tower. The response was slow in coming, and informal, but the parallel row of lights sparkled in the near distance, outlining a runway that was much longer than the blasted dirt strips she was used to.

"Almost there," she murmured, more to herself than Dale.

"Great." He bit off a curse and she felt another flash of annoyance.

"If you're going to snarl at me every time I open my mouth, this is going to be a very long investigation, Metcalf."

"This from the woman who's called me a 'slimy toad' whenever she's seen me for the past three months?" His knuckles whitened. "You wanted happily ever after. I wanted to be friends. The two don't mix, Tansy."

It still hurt that their breakup hadn't crushed him like it had crushed her. Then again, that was part of the problem. "Never mind," she snapped. "Forget I was about to suggest a truce. Let's just keep biting each other's heads off and hope the patients don't notice."

The little plane dropped down through the last fifty feet of air and the rocky bulk of the island flashed beneath them. Their airspeed bled from a hundred miles per hour to eighty, then slower.

Dale sighed heavily and reached out a hand as though to touch her, but he didn't. "Tansy, I'm sorry. I don't mean to fight with you. But this is…awkward for me."

The first of the runway lights glinted below the plane and Tansy brought it down expertly, letting the wheels kiss the smooth, shadowed tarmac. "It's awkward because of me. Because of us."

"No." He shook his head. "Or at least, not entirely. It's the island. You see, I was born—"

Crack! A horrendous jolt yanked the control yoke from Tansy's fingers. Her body slammed against the shoulder harness and the plane bottomed out, hard, on the runway.

"Christ!" Dale yelled, grabbing for a handhold. "Hang on!"

No time. There was no time for hanging on. Sparks flashed by the windows, brighter than the sunset. Metal screamed.

"Dale! The landing gear's collapsed!" Fear grabbed Tansy by the throat. Control. She was out of control.

The little plane slid sideways down the runway at almost fifty miles per hour. Metal ground against asphalt, and sparks spewed higher against the dusky sky. She fought the useless yoke for a few seconds before letting it go. She glanced out the cockpit window. There weren't any buildings to hit at the end of the runway, thank God.

Then her stomach dropped. "The runway *ends!*" she shrieked. "Dale! The ocean!"

"Hang on, baby. Hang on!" Somehow, their hands twined together. Their eyes caught and held as the plane slid over the end of the runway and tilted down.

Metal howled. The plane slammed against something. It twisted and fell, bounced, and continued to fall until they hit bottom, hard.

Tansy's head smacked into the side window.

First, she saw watery stars.

Then she saw nothing.

Chapter Two

The endless moment of freefall was sickening. Dale's stomach lodged in his throat, then dropped when they hit bottom and Tansy's head cracked into the side window. She sagged against her safety belt.

"Tansy! Tansy, stay with me. I need you to stay with me!" The words were rote, the feeling beneath them anything but. Panic roared in Dale's ears. Then he realized it wasn't just panic.

It was the sound of waves breaking on the plane. They'd fallen into the bay. And Tansy was unconscious.

"Damn!" He yanked free of his belt and struggled to his feet, hunching down in the small cockpit space. The cold, salty water of Lobster Bay splashed around his ankles. God, he hated the ocean.

The floor tilted by degrees as the weight of the engine pulled the front of the plane down. Heart pounding, hands shaking, he glanced out the forward window. In the crimson of twilight, he could see wavelets and greasy, gray water edging up the nose of the plane.

How long until the tower sent help? How long would the little plane float?

Working quickly, he checked Tansy's vitals. "Tansy! Tansy, sweetheart, wake up. We need to get out of here, baby." The endearments slipped out, though he'd rarely used them when they had been a couple. At least not out loud.

How deep was the water just past the landing strip? He didn't remember. He hoped it was shallow. Lobster Bay was tricky that way. But even four feet of water would be too much if he couldn't get them out of the plane before it flooded.

Tansy stirred, and relief rattled through him. He could get her out. He had to get her out.

"Flotation," he muttered, knowing that HFH stocked their planes with life jackets as well as the standard cushions. He bypassed the field equipment crammed in the back and yanked the jackets from their compartment. His hands were still shaking. What was wrong with him?

"You've worked outbreaks in Tehru and terrorist bombings in the Middle East," he reprimanded himself. "Two people in a sinking plane should be a piece of cake." He stilled his hands by force of will, but he couldn't stop the lurch of his heart when he returned to Tansy's side and she opened her eyes.

The knowledge hit him like a fist to the gut. This wasn't a stranger in Tehru or the Middle East. This was Tansy.

And that made all the difference.

"Dale? What—?" Pain and sudden comprehension clouded her eyes. "We crashed. The landing gear broke." She turned her head towards the storage space and winced. "We've got to grab the field kits and get out of here."

"Put this on first," he ordered, helping her into the jacket over her protests. "We're in the water and I don't know how long we'll float. Forget about the equipment."

"The hell I will. We have an outbreak to work." Listing to one side as the plane sagged beneath her, Tansy stumbled to the cargo area. She fumbled with the straps securing their instruments. "The cases are shockproof and rigged to float. We'll get as many as we can out the door before we jump."

The floor tilted even further and water surged up to cover most of the cockpit window, blocking out the bloody light of dusk. Dale cursed under his breath. "There's no time for the equipment, Tansy! Let's get the hell out of here."

"We've got time. Help me with this," she demanded.

He clenched his teeth. *Stubborn.* She'd always been stubborn, and more concerned with the patients' safety than her own. At times it scared him and drove him crazy. Other times it made him proud.

This was one of those crazy times.

"We're getting out. Now." In the near-blackness, he looped an arm around her waist and dragged her to the door, grimacing when the floor tilted beneath his feet and metal groaned sickeningly.

The plane was rolling in the water.

"Get the door!" she yelled, finally ready to abandon the equipment. "We're going down!"

"Hurry!" Dale yanked his jacket over his head and tried to help her crank the door release. In a flash, he imagined sinking to the bottom of the ocean with Tansy, trapped in the half-open cockpit. Drowned. Like his parents. "No!" he shouted, and jammed his shoulder against the door.

It cracked open, followed by a gush of water.

"Dale!" Tansy grabbed for him when he lost his footing and went down between the angled seats.

He bobbed up and spat a mouthful of cold, salty water. "Go! Get the hell out of here."

"Not without you," she yelled back. "Come on, we'll jump together and swim away."

Dale knew there'd be suction when the plane went down. They had to get away, and fast. He scrambled to the door, kicking a pair of floating equipment cases out of the way, and boosted Tansy out the door as a wave crested over the plane and swamped the cockpit.

He choked, spitting more seawater. God, he hated the taste.

"Dale, come on. Hurry! I don't think it'll float much longer."

He hauled himself through and jumped. His foot slipped on wet metal and he landed almost in the plane's shadow. The water was cold and harsh.

Like coming home.

Striking out hard, he saw Tansy paddling for all she was worth. Not fast enough.

He was a strong swimmer. He'd had to be, growing up on an island with one of the highest lost-at-sea rates in the Northeast. He grabbed Tansy's jacket and struck out for the beach, hauling her along over her feeble protests. The lights on shore slowly grew closer, though part of him wished they wouldn't.

Halfway there, he heard the unforgettable *hiss-chug* sound of a lobster boat's engine. He tamped down the memories and lifted an arm to the shabby-looking vessel that slowly approached out of the twilight. "Over here!"

"'Hoy there, did everyone make it out?" The man's voice was muffled by wind and wave, but it sounded familiar.

If he weren't already freezing wet, Dale might have shivered as childhood ghosts crammed his brain in a sudden rush. He blinked against them and focused on the cold, hard water and the woman beside him. He raised his voice and called, "Yes. Everyone's out."

It was a lucky thing, too, he thought as the last slice of wing disappeared into the oily, black sea. The water just beyond the runway must be deeper than he remembered, or else the tide was running high. He felt a twinge of remorse for the field kits that had seen them through so many tough assignments, so many exotic locales. The cases were waterproof, but he doubted they were *that* waterproof.

"Hang tight," the helmsman shouted over the noise of the waves and the motor, "we'll have you out of there in a jiffy." The near-derelict boat lurched through the surf and Dale could just read the faded name on its bow. *Churchill IV.*

The name brought a twist of guilt. Dale had promised his parents' friend, Walter Churchill, that once he left the island he'd make a new life for himself and never look back. Well, he was back, and so far it had been a hell of a homecoming.

"Climb aboard, you two. What the heck happened to your plane?" The helmsman steered the *Churchill IV* in close, and another rain-suited figure leaned over and tossed a thick, greasy rope.

"We crashed," Dale answered shortly, though he wanted to know the same thing. One moment, Tansy had been landing as deftly as ever, and the next, the plane was sliding down the runway on its belly.

It made no sense.

He helped her aboard, then scrambled into the boat in a motion that came back easily after all these years. He checked on Tansy. She was pale and shivering, though the men had wrapped her in a coarse, soggy wool blanket. "You okay?"

"Never better," she answered with a crooked smile that squeezed his chest.

Her aplomb was ruined by a thin trickle of blood from a cut on her temple, and the fine tremble of her lower lip. He took a step towards her. "Tansy—"

"I'm fine, Dale. Really." She leaned away.

He knelt down in front of her and took her chilled hands in his own. "Tans—"

She pulled free and stood as the helmsman gestured his companion to the wheel and strode over. The boat's running lights picked out the glittering tracks of salt spray that trickled down his yellow rain suit. A billed hood cast the man's face in deep shadow, but there was something familiar about the rolling walk, the wide, powerful shoulders. A chill skittered through Dale.

Letters and a phone call hadn't prepared him for this. Not really.

The slickered figure lifted a hand and pushed back his hood to reveal a shock of white-blond hair above a weather-beaten face that might once have been pale. The man's tired blue eyes were clear, but dulled with worry. Dale steeled himself to shake the proffered hand. "Mickey." He saw the face of a boy beneath that of the man. "It's been a long time."

"Welcome home, Cousin Dale." Mick nodded and glanced down at Tansy, who sagged against the railing. "And you'd be Dr. Whitmore. Welcome to Lobster Island. I'm sorry for your plane, but thank God you're both all right."

Dale let the voice wash over him as he tried to fit Mickey's image to the memories he'd carried for fifteen years. They'd been as close as brothers until the day Dale's family had gone down in a ferocious spring storm, leaving the seventeen-year-old at the mercy of his grief-maddened uncle.

Trask. Even the memory of the name brought impotent rage.

"I see some debris. I'll bring her around to it," the other slickered man called, interrupting the memory, though not the anger.

"Some of the cases may have washed out of the plane," Dale said harshly, trying to find his doctor's focus. *The job,* he thought. *Focus on the job.* "Pick up as much of the equipment as you can. We'll need it to investigate your shellfish poisoning."

At his elbow, Tansy was ghost-white. Guilt seared through him, layered atop the anger. He should have told her about the island. He should have prepared her better for the shock of learning that this poor, wretched place had once been his home. That these people were his family, such as it was.

Mick muttered a dark curse at the mention of the outbreak. "It's bad, or I wouldn't have asked you to come. We've had three deaths since I called, and another two sick, including the mayor and the sheriff."

Dread curled through Dale, though he hid it deep down with all the other emotions.

"That's impossible," Tansy said after a moment. "PSP isn't fatal, and certainly not in those numbers." Dale could see her mind working.

Personal problems, plane crashes, the cold and the wet faded to the background as his mind clicked over to field mode alongside hers. "You've had more cases?" he asked. "I thought the fisheries people locked down all your lobster traps."

Mickey cursed and jerked his chin toward the dock, dark in the gathering twilight. Black, boat-shaped shadows bobbed gently at their moorings. "The fleet hasn't put to sea in over a week. The catches were bad after the spring storms, but this is a disaster. If we don't get the docks open, the whole island will be hungry by winter. That's why I asked you to come." He glanced out to the end of the marked runway. The landing lights shone bright in the darkness. "Though you almost didn't make it. What the hell happened?"

Tansy answered with a tiny quiver in her voice. "It was like the landing gear...collapsed. Or maybe it fell off. But that doesn't make sense. Landing gear doesn't just fall off."

A shiver started deep in Dale's gut. No, landing gear didn't just fall off.

Not unless it had help.

IT WAS RIDICULOUS, TANSY knew, to think the crash had been anything but an accident. Accidents happened. A pothole in the runway could have snapped a weakened strut. She might have missed a loose nut in her preflight check, or a bolt could have sheared.

But that didn't explain why both wheels failed at once.

She glanced over at Dale, deep in conversation with his *cousin,* and she felt like Alice down the rabbit hole. She didn't understand what was happening. Chillier than a corpse, she pulled the wet wool blanket tighter. *Control.* She wasn't in control of the situation. *Knowledge is power.* She knew nothing. And her head hurt like hell.

When they reached the dock, Dale jumped from the wet, unsteady boat with a practiced motion that made him look like someone other than the man she'd known for so long, the man she'd once thought herself in love with. He took her hand and helped her stumble onto the dock with a good deal less grace than he'd shown.

"Come on. We'll go to the motel and scrounge some dry clothes." His voice was almost the same, but she knew the man beside her even less than she'd known him when they had been lovers. Now, his perfectly groomed hair was plastered to his skull with salt water. The fine linen shirt, monogrammed at the cuff and collar, was ripped askew, and she could see the shadowy old tattoo she'd always assumed was a scorpion. She'd had to assume. He'd refused to answer questions about the tattoo. But the scorpion-shadow had never quite meshed with the urbane polish of his Boston self.

In the glare of the lobster boat's running lights, something flickered in the back of his blue eyes. Something uncivilized.

Without really meaning to, Tansy took a step back. "Dale?"

This time it was irritation that sparked in his eyes. "I told you to stay in Boston, Tansy. You don't belong here."

"Neither do you," she countered. "We're here to do a job." But she wasn't sure which of them she was trying to convince. She shivered from the cold, and from the strangeness of it all.

The poised, elegant Dale Metcalf she knew from Boston would have slid an arm around her shoulders and shared his warmth—though not his heart. The stranger he'd become the moment he set foot on Lobster Island merely turned away and walked toward shore, calling over his shoulder, "Come on. Let's get dry. Then we'll figure out how to get you home."

"I'm not going home," she yelled back through chattering teeth. "We have a job to do."

"You're going back to Boston and that's final. I don't want you here."

Tansy flinched. They'd been broken up for three months now. The thought that he didn't want her shouldn't hurt anymore.

She heard the crinkle of a rubber rain suit and felt a hand on her shoulder. "Come on, Dr. Whitmore. Let's get you inside and dried off. That cut on your head should be seen to, as well."

Miserable from the cold, sick with fear and plagued by an otherworldly feeling, Tansy nodded mutely and followed Dale's cousin to a windowless old jeep.

The men loaded eight salvaged equipment cases into the vehicle, completely filling the back. Dale climbed in the front and held out a hand. "Come on. You can ride with me." He patted one knee, though his eyes told her he wished there was another way.

Tansy stalled. They'd ridden sandwiched together in a hundred military vehicles, before and after becoming lovers. With only one or two transports for the HFH equipment and crew, there was rarely room for comfort. It had never bothered her before. It shouldn't bother her now.

But it did.

Dale saw her hesitation and snapped, "Don't be foolish. You're freezing. Get in. I won't touch you."

But it was a hard promise to keep when the jeep rocked along the bumpy dirt road and jostled them against each other. After a few minutes, his arms encircled her and pulled her back against his chest.

"Relax," he whispered. "It's nothing personal. We'll be at the motel soon."

It's nothing personal. Tansy cursed the surge of hurt, and hated him for not understanding that it *was* personal. Everything between them was too personal, and not personal enough. It had been personal when they'd become lovers on a thin pallet in Tehru. It had been personal when they'd moved in together on assignment. And it had been *very* personal when he'd drawn away from her every time they returned to home base.

Eventually, she'd realized he wasn't letting her in any deeper. Then she'd seen the signs her mother had warned her about. The frequent, unexplained absences. The furtive phone calls. The emotional withdrawal.

When she'd accused him of finding someone else,

he hadn't denied it. He'd let her walk out and he hadn't come after her. That alone had proven Eva Whitmore's point. Either you knew a man inside and out or you didn't. And if you didn't, you were in for a nasty surprise.

The jeep bumped along, and Tansy realized she'd unconsciously relaxed against Dale, sinking into the familiar spots where they fit together so well. Not strong enough to pull away, she sighed and turned her attention to the view. They passed a row of small cottages that might have been pretty once upon a time. Now, paint peeled from the clapboards and fell into weed-choked planting beds. An empty swing dangled from a tree. The whole area was deserted. Depressed.

Tansy thought it strange to find parallels between an island off Maine and the shattered Third World villages they so often visited for HFH. But the island, like the man, was a surprise. She'd envisioned a quaint old New England fishing village with a healthy tourist trade. This poor, dispirited place was anything but. It might have been charming once, might have been picturesque.

Now, it was just dreary. Dale's cousin, Mickey, had mentioned a recent stretch of bad lobstering. She bet it had been going on longer than that.

Automatically, she scanned the area, registering the details of the outbreak location. The familiar action soothed her, distanced her from the feel of the man wrapped around her and the memory of the roughest landing of her piloting career.

Why the hell had the landing gear snapped? As soon as she dried off, she'd call the FAA. There would be an investigation, and an answer.

A sudden lurch of the jeep threw her against Dale's arm and she felt the brush of his thumb along one breast like wildfire. She stifled a gasp as her flesh tightened, and she cursed the flood of wet warmth that swirled at his touch. Her body, it appeared, hadn't forgotten Dale any more than her heart had.

"Sorry." He moved his hand and shifted in his seat, and she became aware that hers wasn't the only body with a memory. She could feel him, hard and ready, against her buttocks. And, God help her, she wanted him with a deep, insistent pulse she hadn't managed to conquer in the time they'd been apart.

She was no better than her mother, willing to accept so much less than she deserved because of an illusion of love.

They bumped past a low collection of cottages with a No Vacancy sign and a few cars in the lot. "Turn in here," Dale snapped, his voice rough with a tone that sent a ripple of memory through her. "I left a message reserving rooms."

Rooms, plural. Tansy hated the flash of disappointment. Of course they weren't staying together. They were broken up. Finished. She was only on the island because HFH management had insisted Dale take his partner. Tansy thought she might strangle her boss when she got home, which would be sooner than later, if Dale got his way.

Home. It was tempting. She was out of her depth, not in control of the situation. But at the same time, it was clear the outbreak wasn't as small an issue as she'd thought. If patients were dying, if people needed her, she'd stay.

Especially since her plane was at the bottom of the ocean.

Chilled, she leaned back against Dale. His arm tightened across her waist as Mickey passed the motel and said, "Sorry, there aren't any vacancies." He turned onto a dirt track, barely visible in the thin headlight beams. Stunted island trees closed in, reaching soggy branches toward the travelers. "The clinic is too small for all the patients. We're using the motel as a hospital, and the only available room is being rented by a big-shot real estate developer named Roberts."

She felt Dale's body tense. "Where are we sleeping, then?"

In Tehru they had picked the dying up off the streets, carried them into the crumbling hotel rooms and treated them on the beds. The HFH doctors had slept on the floors when they'd slept at all. The lodgings weren't important. The patients were.

So why did Dale sound upset? Why was his body tense beneath hers? She looked back over her shoulder and saw his eyes dart from the road to the passing land, as though he wanted to look around but couldn't bear to.

"Your uncle kept the place up," Mickey said, turning into a narrow drive, toward a sprawling house that looked a few degrees better maintained than the cottages near the water. "Painted it every few years and kept the utilities going, just in case."

Just in case what? Tansy wanted to ask, but she choked it down.

Fear and curiosity battled with a growing sense of disillusionment as she realized how much of himself Dale had kept hidden. How little he'd really trusted her.

How little he had loved her.

"I couldn't care less what Trask has or hasn't done." The chill in Dale's tone reminded Tansy of the times she'd pushed him for more and he'd given her less. Cold. He could be so cold.

And she was so confused. What the hell was going on here?

She slid from the jeep and stumbled in a muddy rut. Dale caught her elbow and propped her up. When her feet were steady, he stepped away, attention focused on the cousin, who could have been his weather-beaten twin.

Mickey shook his head. "Your uncle has changed, Dale. I swear it. He's sorry for what he did back then. You should talk to him."

"Not if my life depended on it." The uncivilized spark crackled in Dale's eyes and his voice heated a degree. "Not even if he was dying."

Mickey stared at him for a long moment before nodding. "If you say so." He touched Dale's shoulder briefly, and something akin to regret flickered in

Mickey's faded blue eyes. "There's no agenda here, Cousin. I wouldn't have asked you to come back if I had another choice. And I wouldn't make you stay in this house if there was someplace better. But there isn't, unless you want to stay at Churchill's mansion."

"No," Dale said flatly, staring up at the house. "No, this is fine." He dipped a hand into his pocket, and Tansy saw his fingers work. It was a habit he never seemed aware of. She'd come close to searching his pockets once, to find out what sort of talisman he carried, but she'd stopped herself. That was her mother's game, not hers.

Mickey glanced at his watch and jerked his head toward the sagging porch. "Go on in and get showered and changed. My wife, Libby, left you some basics—towels, clothes, a few odds and ends. Our doctor, Dr. Hazel, will meet you at the motel to go over the patients when you're ready."

As Mickey backed the jeep down the narrow trail, Tansy's confusion and anger tumbled together in a righteous buzz. Still feeling Dale's touch on her flesh, and hating the frigid control he used like a shield, she rounded on him. "What the *hell* is—"

"Later," he interrupted with a short, chopping motion of his hand and a hard look in his eye that sent her back a step. "I'll explain later." He paused, and his eyes softened into something more familiar. Something she almost understood. Something that tugged at her and made her wish things were different. "Let's go inside and get warmed up. I want to have a look at that bump on your head, too. You may need a stitch."

"It's fine. And if I needed a stitch, I'd do it my-self," she replied, feeling the adrenaline and the fear, the cold and the confusion, all catching up to her at once. "Your sutures are lousy. And don't think you're getting out of an explanation, Metcalf."

His eyes softened further, though something dangerous still lurked at the back. "Atta girl. Come on."

He led her up the porch. A hollowed-out shingle near the scratched brass mailbox yielded a key that slipped easily into the simple lock. The faded plaque beside the door contained a single word.

Metcalf.

As she passed through the door into a bare hall-way, she murmured, "Welcome home, Dale."

She got a pithy curse in reply. For some reason, it made her smile. But when she turned, she found him watching her with cold, angry eyes.

"This isn't a joke, Tansy. You don't belong here. There are things going on that you have no part of, and I don't want you hurt."

Though his words and expression were hard, she couldn't help the quick lift of her heart. He cared what happened to her. The hot, wanting pulse re-turned. "Oh? I assumed you didn't want me along be-cause of what happened between us."

Emotion, or maybe desire, flared hot in his eyes, then iced as quickly as it had sparked. "Don't fool yourself. There is no 'us' anymore." He turned away and toed a pile of towels and clothes near the stair-case. "The shower's the second door on the right. The water takes a few minutes to warm up."

Then he walked away, leaving only an echo of footsteps on dry floorboards to mark his presence. Tansy dropped her salty, aching face into her hands.

That was what she'd wanted. No regrets, no hard feelings. Nothing between them. He hadn't been able to give her what she needed, and they'd parted ways. Simple, right?

But there was nothing simple about the ache in her heart. There was nothing simple about the landing gear ripping off, or about an outbreak that was too deadly, too virulent to be shellfish poisoning.

And worst of all, there was nothing simple about the man she'd once thought herself in love with. The playboy doctor who'd looked like a leading actor among extras in the Tehru clinics, and instead had turned out to be…what? A lobsterman's son? The prodigal returned?

She had no idea.

Let me inside, she had pleaded during one of their last real fights. *Don't keep shutting me out. I can't help you if you won't let me in.*

Now, she glanced around the cold, bare entryway, noting where squares of darker wood on the walls suggested pictures long gone. If this was the inside of Dale, she might be better off back in Boston. At least there, she understood the rules.

Here, she understood nothing.

WHEN HE FINALLY HEARD the shower thump to life, Dale pressed his forehead against the cool glass of the kitchen window and closed his eyes. If she had followed him and demanded answers, he wasn't sure what would have come out of his mouth. *There is no "us" anymore.* It was the truth. It *had* to be the truth. Everything that had happened between them was based on a lie.

He wasn't the son of a wealthy Boston shipper. His family's single boat had gone down one night amidst a ferocious spring storm. Or so he'd been told. Nobody, not even the uncle who'd lost his wife in the accident, had wanted to hear Dale's suspicions. The day a drunken Trask had tried to beat the questions out of him was the day seventeen-year-old Dale had fled the island with Walter Churchill's help.

Make yourself into someone else, Churchill had demanded, and sent him off with enough money to do it. *You're better than Lobster Island. You don't belong here.*

But he'd never felt like he belonged where he'd ended up, either. Boston, and the wealthy doctor's life, hadn't sat easily on his shoulders. He'd worked hard to make it fit, even harder when Tansy had come into his life, but the more he tried, the worse the role had pinched.

The shower rumbled overhead, shifting his attention. When he was a child, the noise had made him think of monsters. Now it made him think of Tansy, naked, slick and pink beneath the water. Suddenly, his clothes were more irritating than cold, sticking to the sensitive places. Dale pulled off his ruined shirt and winced as his bumps and bruises throbbed. His quick arousal faded with the memory of those last moments on the runway.

They could have died in the plane crash. They could have sunk to the bottom of the ocean. Dead. Like his parents. And it would have been his fault for bringing Tansy along.

The pipes rattled again, making him think of the shower again. Of Tansy. Without trying, he could imagine steam wreathing her soft, rosy body. Briefly, he let himself remember their time together, let the memory beat back the shadows and the ghosts. The fear.

They had first made love on a pallet in Tehru, barely taking the time to loosen the clothing they wore to bed, to be ready for the next emergency. They had come together in need and despair, wanting to forget the dead and the dying at a time when the outbreak had seemed unbeatable. Then, they'd wanted to feel alive. Later, they'd just wanted to feel. After that first time, they'd stolen moments for quick, furtive couplings when they were too tired to save lives but too wired to sleep.

With the outbreak's source discovered and the disease leveled, they'd headed home, stopping halfway to rent a room with lush plants, marble, brass and silk. And a shower... God, what a shower.

They'd made love in that shower, naked together

for the first time, as perfect for each other as two people could possibly be.

Except that she was perfect for the man Dale had created—wealthy and pedigreed. And that man was nothing more than fiction. If Tansy ever met the real Dale Metcalf, she'd be horrified.

Worse, she'd be disappointed.

And maybe that was why he hadn't fought harder against bringing her. Maybe Lobster Island would do what he had failed to do. Maybe it would kill the attraction between them. Kill the want, and the desperate kick of his heart every time he saw her.

He stepped out of his ruined shoes and eyed the pile of clothes Mickey's wife had left beside a flashlight and a small box of staples. He scowled at the worn jeans and the rough Irish-knit sweater. Dr. Metcalf, infectious disease specialist, didn't own jeans or bulky sweaters. But he'd grown up in them. Shrugging, he scooped the warm clothes off the floor near the stairs and set his foot on the lowest tread.

With the motion, his blood buzzed, and emotions, those things he so often avoided, threatened to swamp him. He'd never needed Tansy's quiet strength more than he did right now. And he had no right to it.

Did he dare go up? If he paused outside the bathroom door and heard her singing in the low contralto that never failed to set his body afire, would he have the strength to keep walking?

Dr. Metcalf would have the strength to walk by,

just as he'd had the nobility to push her away. But Dale Metcalf, lobsterman's brat, knew nothing of nobility. He knew nothing of honor or civility, but he knew about desire. About the want that had chased through his veins ever since he'd held Tansy in his lap on the drive over and remembered how she smelled. How she tasted.

How she felt wrapped around him. Needing him. Loving him.

Oh, yes. He knew about those things. And the memory burned in his lungs. Fighting for strength, for sanity, he turned away from temptation.

And heard Tansy scream.

Chapter Three

"Dale! Dale, get up here! *Hurry!*" The terror in her voice kicked him up the stairs at a dead run. He'd never heard Tansy scream before. Ever.

Moving fast, he shouldered open the door and slid to a halt at the sight of her perfect, round derriere. She was leaning out the bathroom window, dripping on the floor.

"Tans?" He plunged into the small, steamy room, slapped the shower off and heard rustling thumps down below.

There was someone outside.

"Dale!" She turned, clutching a towel to her chest. "There was a man looking in the window. He was *watching me!* What the hell is going on here?"

The tree.

"Damn it!" He brushed her aside and threw a leg out the window. It had been fifteen years since the last time he'd snuck away from Trask and broken into his old house, but the tree still stood outside the bathroom window. And the sounds of running footsteps below told him it was still strong enough for climbing.

"Omigod, what are you doing?" Her voice bordered on shrill, but he didn't pause.

He grabbed the gutter and swung a leg over to the thickest limb. The motions came back easily, and within seconds he was halfway down the tree. A shadow of movement from the garden gate caught his eye. "Stay put," he yelled to her. "I'll be right back." He dropped to the ground and sprinted for the lane that ran behind his mother's overgrown garden.

There were two sets of footsteps and a frantic shout of, "Hurry! Jeez, here he comes!" from the running shadows.

Dale chose the one on the left and made a leaping tackle. He and his quarry went down in the lane amidst a flurry of arms and legs. A pointy elbow cracked Dale under the chin and he swore, realizing he'd landed on maybe fifty pounds of skinny kid.

"Quit!" he barked, and the squirming subsided. A nearby rustle told him the other boy hadn't gone far, so he rolled off his captive. Sitting in the dirt, Dale shook his head. "What do you think you're doing, looking in while a lady's showering? Does your ma know about this?"

Blue eyes widened beneath tousled white-blond hair. Moonlight washed the kid to ghost-pale. "You're not going to tell her, are you, mister? I swear we didn't mean nothing by it. We climb up that old tree sometimes and peek in the window of the haunted house. We didn't think there was anyone in there, honest!"

"And the lights didn't give you a clue?" Dale asked sternly, wondering when his boyhood home had gained a ghost.

The blond head shook vigorously. "It's haunted. I told you. Sometimes there are lights in there but nobody's home. We thought it was the ghosts, and I dared Eddie to go look and he dared me right back, and..." He trailed off and finally shrugged. "We thought the lady might be a ghost. Then she screamed and you came running... Hey, what're you doing in there, anyway? That house belongs to my daddy's cousin!"

Mickey. Dale's throat closed. Mick's infrequent letters had mentioned his sons, but the boys hadn't seemed real when Dale had been sitting in his cubbyhole office in Boston General, reading the piles of mail that gathered dust while he was on assignment. But this boy was so much more than words on a piece of paper. He was a little person who looked like Mickey.

At a second furtive rustle, Dale said, "You can come on out. I might not even tell your ma."

The second boy, a smaller version of the first, crept from a shadowy beach plum and crouched at his brother's side. "Sorry, mister. We didn't mean to scare the lady. DJ thought she was a ghost."

DJ. The elder of the two was named Dale John. Mickey had mentioned it in passing, but Dale hadn't given it much thought.

Now, he sat stunned. He had family. How had he forgotten that? Or had he known it all along and not wanted to deal with the responsibilities that went with it? Trask had taught him that connections meant loss. Hurt. Anger.

Life in Boston was easier without all of those things.

A loud rustle and a series of thumps startled the boys, who squeaked in alarm and backpedaled on their skinny butts. A circle of yellow light slipped through the garden gate, followed by the shape of a woman.

"Dale?"

"Over here, Tans," he called. "I caught your Peeping Toms."

"Toms?" The flashlight beam bounced toward them. "As in, more than one?"

Dale stood and hauled the boys to their feet, feeling the adrenaline level out, leaving confusion behind. "Yeah. But they didn't mean any harm. They thought you were a ghost."

She'd changed into jeans and a hand-knit sweater like the one he was wearing. Dale felt the boys relax at his side when she flicked the beam of light to her own face. "Nope," she said, "no ghost, though they did almost scare me to death." She leaned down and offered a hand. "I'm Tansy."

In the yellow light, the boys' hair shone brighter, their eyes seemed bluer. The younger one shook Tansy's hand. "I'm Eddie and my stomach feels funny."

The older boy frowned. "I'm DJ, and don't listen to him, his stomach always feels funny." Then he scuffed the dirt with his toe. "Sorry we scared you, lady. We didn't think there was anyone in the house, honest. Don't tell Ma, okay?"

Dale had often heard similar words from Mickey when they'd been caught committing some boyhood crime or another.

He swallowed. "Run on home now, boys. Miss Tansy and I have work to do." His voice cracked but he didn't care. "I'll be by to talk to your pa later, but don't worry. This'll be our secret."

When they were gone, Tansy clicked off the flashlight. They stood awkwardly in the darkness until she finally said the words he'd been dreading. "I thought you were a rich kid from Boston."

He'd known it would hurt her to learn he was a fraud. He'd imagined how the disappointment would cross her face, and how she would rally quickly and try to pretend his past didn't matter when they both knew it did. He'd known all that.

What he hadn't known was how hard it would be to admit that it had all been a lie.

He sighed and tried to make the first cut a clean, lethal one. "That's what you were supposed to think, Tansy. That's what everyone thought." When she didn't answer, he took the flashlight, clicked it on and gestured back to the house. "Let's go inside."

But as they walked in silence, Dale realized he didn't want to talk about it. He didn't know what to say. They entered the kitchen and Tansy returned the flashlight to the box Libby had left.

After a moment, she turned to him. "Just tell me this, Dale. Who the hell are you?"

He opened his mouth to answer, but nothing came out. At Boston General, he knew who he was. On assignment, he knew. But on Lobster Island?

He had no idea.

THE SILENCE STRETCHED until Tansy began to doubt Dale was going to speak at all. Then she saw his eyes flickering the way they did when he was mentally flipping through diagnoses and treatment options. He was trying to choose an answer.

"Never mind." She held up a hand to stop the lie. It would be one of many, she now realized, just as she now understood that the man she'd fallen in love with was nothing more than a figment of her imagination. Like mother, like daughter. Whitmore women fell for the schemers. She took a hurting breath that barely moved the stone-heavy pressure on her chest. "Tell me the truth or nothing, okay, Dale? You owe me that much."

When he remained silent, she nodded and hid the disappointment down deep, alongside most of the memories of her father. "Fine. I'll check the lab equipment and see what's salvageable. You shower, and then we can head for the motel clinic. The sooner we solve this outbreak, the sooner we can get out of here." The sooner she could request to be transferred away from Boston. Away from Dale.

She would not repeat her mother's mistakes.

When he didn't answer, she turned toward the salt-encrusted cases piled in the hallway.

"Tansy." His quiet word brought her up short, but she didn't look back. She didn't want to see his gleaming blue eyes. Didn't want to remember how his features had been mirrored in the faces of those two boys out in the lane.

Didn't want to think that she'd once imagined their sons looking just like that.

"It's okay, Dale," she finally said. "I can handle it." She crouched down near the pile of equipment and waved at the stairs, hiding her face so he wouldn't see the hurt. "Go shower. We need to see our patients."

The job. Concentrate on the job. Medicine gave her control. Research told her the truth.

Dale didn't.

He headed for the stairs, pulling the bulky sweater off over his head as he walked. He stopped near her in the narrow hallway, and Tansy was enveloped in familiar warmth. Only this time, it was laced with something new. Something hotter and harder than the pull she'd felt toward Dale Metcalf, playboy, or even Dr. Metcalf, field researcher.

Her whole relationship with Dale had been based on a lie, yet she still wanted him.

Afraid if she looked into his eyes he'd see the hunger, she stared straight ahead at the place where the sinew and bone of his shoulder gave way to the hard planes of his chest. The scorpion tattoo, blurred with time, dominated her view.

Only it wasn't a scorpion.

She reached out a finger and traced the curve of a tail, the pair of wicked hooked claws. "It's a lobster."

Dale sucked in a breath when she touched him, and his body went rigid. "Aye. It's a lobstah."

And his voice was pure Island.

Startled, she looked up at him. Trapped in the potent blue of his eyes, she didn't move when he stepped closer, crowding her. Tempting her.

"You want to know who I am, Tansy?" He leaned close so he was almost whispering in her ear. "I'll tell you who I'm not. I'm not a prep-school boy, and I'm not a gentleman." She quivered as his words ran across her bare neck and heat coiled in her stomach.

She could turn her head just a fraction, and their lips would touch. She could run and never look back.

In the instant before she made the decision, he made it for her. He stepped away. His muscles were corded with tension and he gripped the banister like a lifeline. "Check the equipment, we leave in ten minutes. And remember, I'm not the Dale Metcalf you thought you knew. The next time I have you up against a wall, I'm not going to back away."

Though the image churned her stomach into sharp, sizzling knots, Tansy rounded on him as he climbed the stairs. "Don't even think you're calling the shots here, Dale. I won't stand for it. I could have died in that plane crash. Don't you think that entitles me to know what the hell is going on?"

"No," he snapped back from the second floor. "I

think it entitles you to a one-way ticket home the second I can arrange it. I knew I shouldn't have let you come with me."

"Let me?" Her voice climbed several octaves, though she wasn't sure why she was fighting the idea. She should want to escape the island. To escape Dale and the insane pull he exerted on her. "Let me? Nobody *let* me do anything, Dale. This is my job, and—"

The slam of the bathroom door cut her off.

"Oooh," she said, popping the first of the cases open. *"Jerk."*

All her life it had been this way. Her father had shared his wealth freely with his only child—as well as his mistresses—but he'd expected her to marry well and bring her husband into the family business. Her mother had nodded and smiled in public, then gone through his pockets at night, weeping over the matchbooks and hotel receipts.

For all Tansy knew, she still did.

They'd been horrified when Tansy had used part of her trust fund to pay for med school and donated the rest to HFH. She'd met Dale on her first assignment. He'd shoved a field pack at her and said, "Dale Metcalf. Glad to have you here. There are two little girls trapped under a beam in the second house on the right. Don't slow me down."

And though she'd later learned—or thought she had—that he came from the same social stratum as her parents, Dale had never coddled her, never expected any less of her than he did from the male doctors. At first, it had been a relief. Then an annoyance when she realized it was because he never let anyone past the brittle outer shell of false charm.

Never let anyone inside.

"Well," she muttered, glancing again at the dark squares of wood on the walls, wondering what story the missing pictures might have told. "I'm inside. Sort of. Now what the hell do I do?"

"Is this a private conversation, or may I intrude?"

Tansy screeched and spun toward the voice, jerking her hands into the attack position she'd been taught before her first overseas assignment. *Go for the eyes and the crotch,* the instructor's voice shouted in her head. *Use any weapon you can find!*

The stranger stumbled back a pace and held his hands up. "Whoa, whoa! Easy there."

She froze, vibrating with a tension she hadn't consciously recognized. Then again, her reaction was understandable. Alice had fallen down the rabbit hole, into the ocean, and come out somewhere on an island populated by Dale Metcalf clones. It hadn't been a banner day up to this point. Considering their next stop was a makeshift clinic where people were dying of a nonfatal disease, she had little hope of it improving.

Especially not with a stranger standing in the kitchen.

She glared at the tall, silver-haired man, and was almost surprised to see that his eyes were brown, not blue. She relaxed a fraction, though she kept her weight on the balls of her feet as she'd been taught. "Who are you and what are you doing here?"

The water cut off upstairs. She raised her voice and called, "Dale? We have company."

The stranger's eyes glinted with approval. "Smart of you, though not necessary. I know you're not alone. I've come to give you and Dale a ride to the clinic." He held out a hand. "I'm Walter Churchill."

Of all the characters she'd met so far in this not-quite-Wonderland, Churchill was the biggest surprise. Cultured, elegant, and turned out in a charcoal suit and burgundy tie, he would have been right at home in one of the chichi clubs in the Theater District near Boston General. He also acted as though she should know him.

Then again, she probably *would* know him if Dale had told her the truth about his past.

Stifling the flash of resentment, she shook the proffered hand. "Dr. Tansy Whitmore. Pleased to meet you." *I think.*

Then she heard movement on the stairs behind her and Dale's quiet, level voice. "Churchill."

She glanced back and her mouth dried to dust when the sight of Dale dressed in jeans and a home-spun sweater drove home just how strange a situation she was in. The borrowed denim clung to his long thighs and lean calves, and rode low at his flat waist. He cocked a hip against the stair handrail and fixed the older man with a look. "How did you get in here?"

A parade of emotions passed across Churchill's face, too quick, too deep for Tansy to read. Finally, he sighed and said, "The kitchen door was open, so I let myself in. I've never needed an invitation before."

Dale flushed and rubbed his unshaven jaw. "Sorry. I'm in a mood. It's good to see you, Churchill."

Tansy had thought herself beyond shock. She was wrong. "Dale? You know this man?" That was a foolish question. Of course Dale knew the stranger, it was becoming clear that he knew everyone on the island.

"Yeah." He glanced down at her. "I promised you an explanation. Well, here's the short version. I was born here. My parents and my aunt died in a boating accident when I was seventeen, and my uncle Trask took it out on me. Churchill was a friend of my parents. He helped me escape to the mainland and put me through college and med school, for which I am eternally grateful."

Yet Tansy noticed little warmth on Dale's face when he scowled down at the older man. She waited a heartbeat. Then another. *Tell me,* she wanted to scream, *tell me more. Let me in!* But the words had never worked before. They weren't likely to now.

Finally, she turned back to the medical instruments. "Fine. Nice to meet you, Mr. Churchill." She slapped the cases shut. "Come on. Let's get over to the clinic."

Ignoring the men, she grabbed two equipment cases at random and hauled them to the front door.

She paused at the sight of the shiny new black SUV in the driveway.

Someone on this island had money, it appeared.

"Frankie will get the rest of your boxes," Churchill murmured behind her as the driver's door opened and an enormous woman in chauffeur's livery emerged to tower over the vehicle. She didn't say a word as she brushed past Tansy and picked up the remainder of the equipment cases in a single load.

The word *Amazon* came to mind. So did *bodyguard*.

Who the hell was this Churchill? Tansy shot Dale a look, but he avoided her silent question by bending to shift one of the cases in the trunk. She scowled and ducked into the SUV when Frankie held the door open. The black interior smelled of new leather and money. A lethal-looking Doberman sat in the front, between the seats. It faced the passengers and curled a tan lip when Tansy slid inside.

She would have preferred a white VW Rabbit with plates that read *I'm late*. That, at least, she would have understood. The feeling that she was headed to the worst sort of tea party intensified, as did the nagging fear and her headache, though the cut on her head had scabbed without needing stitches.

As the vehicle bumped back the way they'd come, Churchill spoke as though resuming an interrupted conversation. "This outbreak business is bad, Dale. Bad. The docks are losing money every day we're closed, and my customers on the mainland are finding other places to buy their lobsters."

Tansy remembered the name Churchill on the bow of the lobster boat. Though it surprised her that Mickey and Churchill both seemed more concerned with the lobstering than the patients, she supposed the inhabitants of Lobster Island must live—and die—by their catches.

"That's why I'm here, Walter. The outbreak isn't typical. There shouldn't be new cases, or as many fatalities. But I'm curious." Dale leaned forward to address the man in the front. As he did so, his hard thigh brushed against Tansy's leg and she moved away, hating the flush of contact. "Why did I hear about this from Mickey? You knew where to find me, and you know I'm a doctor. An outbreak specialist. Why didn't you call me for help?"

Churchill glanced back. "Because until three people died this morning, I thought it was under control. And because I didn't want you coming back here."

Dale cursed. "Because of Trask."

The older man shook his head. "Because of you, Dale. You don't belong here. You never did."

The SUV pulled into the motel parking lot. Anticipation, and perhaps relief, surged through Tansy when she saw an agitated, gesturing crowd gathered around a windowless Jeep. An older woman in wrinkled scrubs dashed out of a motel door and hurried to the crowd.

The scene screamed *medical emergency!* Tansy's pulse jolted. Medicine. Knowledge. She could do this. Here, she could be in control.

She had the door open before the vehicle stopped rolling, HFH training kicking in when nothing else made sense. "Come on, Dale. We have work to do!" Feeling naked without her field rucksack, which had gone down with the plane, she sprinted across the parking lot to the growing crowd.

Behind her, Churchill yelled a question and Dale called back, "Yeah. Call the FAA about the crash and call Zachary Cage at Boston General. Tell him I need more field equipment, clothes and another plane. Pronto."

Intent on the patient, Tansy ignored her partner and pressed through the crowd. When she saw the man at its center, she stopped dead.

Mickey.

She held up a hand to stop Dale, but she was too late to spare him the sight of his cousin cradling a small child to his chest. Tears ran down the lobsterman's wrinkled, wind-burned cheeks.

"Mick, you have to give Eddie to me *now.*" The older woman in the scrubs—Tansy guessed she was Dr. Hazel—pried at the lobsterman's fingers. "He's in respiratory arrest. You have to let me help him breathe."

Dale made a low sound, almost that of an animal in pain. Hurting for him, hoping it wasn't too late, Tansy stepped forward. Hands outstretched, she waited until Dale's cousin focused on her. "Mickey, remember me? I'm Dr. Whitmore. We're here to help. You need to let us help Eddie now. He needs to be on a respirator." She refused to admit it might already be too late for the little boy who'd complained of stomach pains not an hour earlier.

She'd missed it. How had she missed it?

The torture in Mickey's face clawed at her heart. The lobsterman shook his head. "I've got to protect him. He's mine."

Then Dale nudged her aside. "I've got him, Mick. I'll fix him for you. I promise. Trust me." He reached for the limp body and Mickey finally handed the boy over.

"He's sick, Dale. My boy's sick. You said nobody else would get sick once we stopped lobstering. But my Eddie's sick."

"Get him inside Unit 2," Dr. Hazel ordered, clearing a path through the murmuring crowd. "There's a respirator in there for him."

Cradling his precious cargo, Dale jogged to the motel room behind Hazel. Tansy followed in his wake, her brain already churning with lists of diseases that looked like PSP but weren't. Deadly diseases.

Focused on the child and the need to hurry, she almost missed the small object that dropped from Eddie's tiny hand. She scooped it up on the run. It was a dark-colored rock, the sort of thing boys picked up as treasures. Thinking he might want it back if, no *when,* he recovered, she shoved it in the pocket of her borrowed jeans.

The door to Unit 1 opened and a dark-haired man poked his head out. As they rushed by, Tansy caught a flash of capped teeth and navy trousers.

"Hey, Hazel," the man called, seeming oblivious that Dale was giving Eddie mouth-to-mouth as they hurried into Unit 2, "is the mayor well enough to talk yet? I need to get these sales agreements signed, and—"

Tansy slammed the door behind them, cutting him off midsentence. *Big-shot real-estate developer,* Mickey had said. Well, he could go build condos in hell for all she cared. They had a life to save.

"How long has he been down?" Dale snapped as he placed the limp body on the edge of a motel bed.

"Not long. He'd just stopped breathing when you arrived. We should be okay." Hazel expertly fitted a tube into the boy's throat and passed Dale the hand-held apparatus. "You bag him, I'll finish setting up the respirator." She glanced at Tansy. "I'm Hazel Dodd, and I'm very glad you're here. Walter Churchill asked for help a week ago, but the feds didn't have anyone to send. Thank God Trask knew who to ask."

"Mickey contacted me," Dale said curtly, squeezing the bag in shallow puffs to inflate Eddie's small lungs just enough but not too much. "Not Trask."

"Because I knew you'd hang up on me," said an unfamiliar voice from the doorway.

Tansy whirled. An older man stood at the threshold, clutching a wool cap in his hands. Blond and blue-eyed, he could've passed as Dale's father.

Or his uncle.

"Get him out of here." Dale's voice was as cold

as she'd ever heard it. "Now." But there was an echo of something else. Something young and wistful.

Trask backed up a pace. His eyes flicked to Hazel, then slid away. He clenched his jaw. "I'll go. But I wanted to say—"

"I don't care what you wanted to say," Dale interrupted. One of his hands carefully bagged the small child, keeping him alive while Hazel adjusted the respirator. Dale's other hand stabbed toward the door. "Get out."

"I want to apologize, boy. You could at least hear what I have to say." Trask's voice roughened and he twisted the cap in his hands.

Tansy expected Dale to shut the other man out, as he'd shut her out so many times before. End the conversation. Walk away. In Dale's world, silence was easier than sharing.

But as Hazel took over the bag and transferred Eddie to the mechanical respirator, Dale stayed put and swallowed, hard. "Apologize for which part? Are you sorry you blamed me for Aunt Sue's death? Sorry you hated me? Or are you sorry that I stayed as long as I did?"

A muscle pulsed in Trask's jaw and his faded blue eyes narrowed. "Watch your mouth, boy. I did my duty by you." When Dale snorted, Trask took a step forward, then stopped himself and cursed. "Never mind. It's history. If you don't want to hear it, that's your choice, but I'll say it anyway. I think you were right."

Dale went still. "Right about what?"

Trask glanced over his shoulder at the crowd outside, stepped inside the motel room and shut the door. "I didn't listen fifteen years ago because I couldn't think of anything but Suzie. But things have been happening, Dale. Strange things."

"What things?" Dale swallowed with an audible click. "What are you saying?"

Trask took a deep breath, glanced at the child on the bed and said, "I think you were right. I think Suzie and your parents may have been murdered."

Chapter Four

Murdered. Though a shock, the word clicked in Dale's head, unlocking a hurricane of jumbled suspicions, fears and resentments. But not grief, not really. The grief had been washed out of him years ago. Or else he'd pushed it so far down he couldn't even find it anymore.

But *murder?*

He turned away on the pretext of checking Eddie's pulse. It was steady. Saxitoxin, the main poison of PSP, didn't usually stop the heart. The rare death came from system failure. The first symptoms of shellfish poisoning were a faint tingling of the mouth and fingertips, sometimes with a stomachache, and—

And he was hiding behind the job. Funny, he usually left that to Tansy.

"He's breathing." Hazel's competent hands gestured Dale away from the patient. "All we can do now is wait until his body clears the toxin." *Or he dies,* was the unspoken end to her sentence. "You'll want to see the other patients, and my notes. But it can wait if you'd like a moment with your uncle."

First Mickey. Then Walter Churchill. Now Trask. Dale didn't think he could handle another reunion. Even if he could, the last person he'd pick for a welcome home party was the uncle who'd crawled into a bottle the night the *Curly Sue* had gone down with all hands aboard.

Seventeen-year-old Dale had needed Trask's compassion, if not his love. Thirty-two-year-old Dr. Metcalf wanted nothing to do with either. He turned away. "No need. Let's see the other patients."

"Dale…" Hazel touched his sleeve. "Maybe if you just listened—"

"No." He glared over his shoulder, trying not to see how drained his uncle looked. How much deeper the lines beside his mouth cut, how his hair had bleached to an old man's white. "I don't need to listen. Churchill showed me where the flotsam from the *Curly Sue* came ashore. And Trask assured me—with his fists, when necessary—that it was nothing more than an accident. Well, guess what? I'm a believer. Lobstering's a tough business, and boats go down. Isn't that what you told me, Trask? Aunt Sue and my parents sank. Period. End of story." Dale pointed to the door. "I'd like you to leave now so my colleagues and I can save this boy's life."

He felt a twist of guilt for using little Eddie as leverage, but the pressure building in his chest needed an outlet. If Trask didn't leave, it was going to be him. And though Dale owed the old man for a black eye and a sore jaw, he liked to think he was better than that. He was better than Trask.

Better than Lobster Island.

Finally, he heard rubber boots creak on the cheap carpet. The door closed behind Trask, and Dale let out a breath, felt the tension ease slightly.

"Dale," Hazel said in a quiet, censorious tone, "you should talk to him."

Aware of Tansy standing beside the bed, eyes shadowed with questions mixed together with worry for the boy, Dale clenched his jaw. She shouldn't have to learn about his past like this. He'd been wrong all along.

He should have told her before they'd come to the island. No matter that she hadn't returned his calls the night before they left, he should have pounded on her door until she let him in. He should have told her, made her understand how little she knew him.

How little she would like the man he really was.

"Sorry, Hazel." He shook his head and avoided Tansy's eyes. "I'm here to investigate an outbreak, not have a tearful homecoming in a place that ceased being home fifteen years ago. I'm not here to make peace with a bastard like Trask, and I'm certainly not here to ask questions about a boat that went down when I was a teenager. That's all ancient history." He glanced down at the bed. "My life started the moment I hit the mainland, and it won't continue until I'm back where I belong. So let's get on with this, okay?"

Without another word, Hazel nodded and led the way out into the parking lot. Dale gestured for Tansy to precede him through the door, but she stayed where she was and narrowed her eyes.

In her face he saw the one thing he'd feared all along. Disappointment.

And though he'd always known it would come to this—that she'd hate where he'd come from, what he'd been—Dale couldn't stop the quick slice of pain. He covered it with a scowl. "Come on. We have work to do."

Hazel was waiting for them at the door to Unit 3. With a shimmer of surprise, Dale realized she looked old, too. And smaller than he remembered, though he'd not thought of her in a long, long time. Hazel had returned to the island not long before his parents' deaths, bringing her brand new medical degree to replace Doc Hawley when his boat had capsized off the point.

Doc's body had been recovered, Dale remembered with a twinge of resentment. His kin hadn't been forced to bury an empty box.

"What can you tell us, Dr. Dodd?" Tansy's professional question jerked Dale back to the present. That's where he belonged. In the present, not the past.

"Just Hazel's fine, dear." The island's doctor, who could've gone somewhere else with her Ivy League degree but had insisted on returning to this godforsaken place, pushed open the door and waved the others through. "We've had nine cases so far. Gerald Cohen came to my office last Friday, complaining of a tingling, burning feeling in his fingers and lips. And you know these lobstermen...for him to come see me, it had to have gotten bad. They'll ignore anything short of a severed digit or arterial spurts."

"Is this Mr. Cohen?" Tansy asked as they entered the room.

"No." Hazel's mouth drooped and Dale again noticed how worn she looked. She had to be in her late forties, but she looked a decade past that. She'd been beautiful once. Now she was tired. "Gerry died that night. He went into respiratory arrest around five o'clock and I put him on a ventilator, but it was no good. His heart quit."

Tingling. Burning. Respiratory failure. Cardiac arrest. The symptoms were consistent with PSP, but only a small percentage of shellfish poisonings went into respiratory arrest. Here, it seemed like they all did. It made no sense.

Dale felt the first stirrings of interest. In his anger over Tansy, Trask and the enforced return to Lobster Island, he'd lost sight of their immediate purpose. An outbreak. Gratefully, he let his mind click over to analytical mode. In medicine, as in any investigation, there was little room for emotion. That was one of the reasons the job suited him so perfectly.

"Tell us about this patient," he requested, moving to stand near the bed and gaze down at the young woman lying motionless in it.

"Miranda Davis. Sixteen years old. Her boyfriend,

Curtis, brought her in this morning. She's been on the respirator since noon today."

"So she should be coming out of paralysis in the next few hours," Dale commented. Saxitoxin and the other shellfish poisons usually wore off in half a day.

But Hazel shook her head. "No. I've had patients stay in arrest for twenty-four, even thirty-six hours, and counting. So far, only Traub Daniels has come out of it, and he's breathing on his own but still unconscious. The others died." Hazel took the teen's hand and ran a thumb across a single broken nail. "One patient passed away just an hour ago. Mary Darling. Her baby is only four months old."

Though he'd taught himself to internalize human tragedy and use it to fuel his efforts, Dale couldn't seem to rise above the sight of the teenage girl in the motel bed. Her chest rose and fell in a relentless, unnatural rhythm. He felt Tansy at his side and almost reached for her.

But he didn't. He couldn't.

The pressure on his chest increased and he was grateful that Tansy asked the next question. "You said her boyfriend brought her in. Can we speak with him?"

Isolate the patients. Chart the course of the disease. Identify it. Find the source. Neutralize it. Their job was simple.

And not simple at all.

Hazel shook her head, the lines pulling tighter beside her mouth. "Curtis Flink. He collapsed a half hour after he brought Miranda in. He's in Unit 5. His kidneys are failing."

"This is awful." Tansy pressed her fingertips to her eyes to stop a headache, or perhaps tears.

He'd bet on the headache. The cut on her temple had scabbed over, but he couldn't forget the sight of her lying limply in the pilot's seat, unconscious. He should have left her in Boston. Should have driven her away. She wasn't safe here.

Where the hell had that last thought come from? She was certainly safer in Maine than she'd been in Tehru, and he hadn't been intent on sending her home then.

Focus, Metcalf. Think about the outbreak, not the island. Not Mickey or Trask. Not Churchill. And especially not Tansy. *Do your damn job.*

He turned away from the bed, away from the sight of the girl's chest rising and falling. He brushed past Tansy, ignoring the questions in her eyes, and opened the door. "Come on. Let's go see the boyfriend next."

LET ME INSIDE, TANSY wanted to scream as she followed Dale across the dirt parking lot to Unit 5. *What's going on here? Who are you?* But she knew it would be futile because he had no intention of lowering the walls around his heart.

Stepping inside yet another motel room, Dale asked, "Did he say anything before he collapsed? Did he mention the two of them eating any shellfish? Anything that might have contained lobster, clams, anything?"

The blend of poisons created by red tide blooms accumulated harmlessly in the tissue of shellfish, yet was poisonous to humans. Worse, it wasn't disabled by cooking, a common misconception that was the source of many cases of PSP.

Standing beside the bed of a dark-haired young man hooked to a ventilator and a dialysis machine, Hazel shook her head. "He was pretty altered when he came in, kept mumbling about lightning bolts indoors and Ali Baba. Maybe he was flashing back on a cartoon? I'm not sure. But I'm sorry. He didn't say anything useful."

Numbness. Tingling. Respiratory arrest. Kidney failure. More than twelve hours to recover. The list of symptoms buzzed inside Tansy's head, almost, but not quite, sounding like PSP.

"What equipment did we rescue?" Dale's voice broke into her thoughts. "And do you think any of it will work?"

Identify the disease. It looked like PSP, but was it really? Though she still jumped a little at the sound of his voice, and the way it seemed to caress the back of her neck with memory and regret, Tansy latched onto the familiar thought patterns of her work as she answered. "We pulled out the portable chromatograph. Is it broken?" She shrugged. "There's only one way to find out."

Though PSP came from a blend of many different poisons, a cocktail specific to each red tide, there were a few core toxins they could screen for using the chromatograph. At least then they could be sure they were dealing with PSP. Then they could make a plan. Find the source.

But just then, a woman's voice yelled from outside. "Dr. Hazel? Dr. Hazel!"

There was a sudden flurry of noise. Wheels sliding on dirt. Agitated shouts. Tansy's stomach dropped and she hoped to hell they had more respirators when the voice shouted, "We've got four more out here, and another two on the way. Dr. Hazel, can you hear me?"

The three doctors looked out into the parking lot and saw chaos. Bodies sprawled in a pickup truck. A woman retching into a plastic garbage can. A small boy climbed out of the cab of the truck, staggered, and fell to his knees, crying.

"God," Tansy breathed, and unconsciously leaned into Dale when she felt him at her shoulder. "This is awful."

"Yeah." He gave her a quick, one-armed hug. "Come on, Tans. We have work to do."

BY THE FOLLOWING AFTERNOON, nearly twenty-four hours later, the flood of new patients had slowed to a trickle. The good news was that they hadn't contracted PSP, merely standard-issue food poisoning that the doctors quickly traced to cans of old tuna used at the island's single diner. Already, the strictures against fishing and lobstering in the waters off the island were pinching into the inhabitants' meager tinned resources.

The bad news was that three of the original PSP patients had died and there didn't seem to be anything the doctors could do about it.

Dale was bone tired. Maybe he was getting old. Maybe he was losing his edge. Or maybe there were too many memories, too many emotions threatening to break through. Whatever the cause, he saw each of the blond patients' faces, and cringed. He heard each of their cries and saw each pair of scared blue eyes, and lost the professional detachment that made him the best of the best.

Tansy had always been able to blend medicine with compassion. At first, he'd mocked her for it. Then, he'd envied her. Now, he didn't know how he felt.

"You okay?" As though summoned by his thoughts, she was at his side, touching him on the shoulder.

"I'm fine," he said shortly, and moved away from her hand and the weakness it represented. But he wasn't fine. Every time he saw an islander's face or heard the broad accent, he was thrown back in time to the days just before his parents' deaths. The days just after.

Tansy waited, and Dale wished he could reach for her. Wished he could talk to her. But he didn't know how. Sharing meant vulnerability. Trask had taught him that.

Finally, she sighed and asked, "Ready for the meeting?"

He nodded. "Yeah, let's go."

They left the patients with Hazel for the night. The young man, Curtis, had died, despite the dialysis and their best efforts to help his kidneys and liver clear the toxin. His girlfriend Miranda was finally breathing on her own, though she hadn't regained consciousness. Both the sheriff and the mayor were nonresponsive—alive only because of the machines that breathed for them.

Little Eddie was still hooked up to a respirator, as well. It had been almost twenty-four hours since he'd collapsed. Too long, but what more could they do? The symptoms made no sense. PSP came from eating tainted shellfish, yet none of the patients had eaten the same foods before they collapsed. How could they fight something that didn't follow the rules?

The fear level on the island was escalating rapidly on the wings of sorrow over lost spouses, lost children.

Lost parents.

At the thought, the word *murder* whispered around the edges of Dale's brain, but he shook off Trask's words. At seventeen, Dale would have given anything to have his uncle believe that his mother wouldn't have gone out on the boat after dark. Now, he couldn't afford to even ask the question. He had an outbreak to solve, and he had to get Tansy back to Boston.

Besides, the proof had been irrefutable. The *Curly Sue* had gone down with all hands aboard. Period.

"None of this makes any sense," Tansy murmured

as they crossed the motel lawn and headed for the small, white building that served as Lobster Island's meeting place.

Dale nodded. "You're right. There's something strange going on."

Which was why he wanted her off the island. Churchill had agreed to arrange a charter for the next day and Dale planned to bundle her onto the plane, kicking and screaming if necessary. Once she was safe on the mainland, he could deal with the rest of it. This was his problem, not hers.

"It's almost as though there's a new, concentrated source of the toxin somewhere on the island." Tansy scowled. "We'd know more if the test had worked."

Salt water had leaked into their centrifuge and fried the hell out of its programming. They hadn't noticed the problem until halfway through purifying the first set of blood samples, and the mistake had set them back by hours. They still didn't know whether they were dealing with PSP or something else.

"Churchill said he'd call for more field kits and some satellite phones," Dale said, not bothering to tell Tansy she'd be gone long before the new equipment arrived, or that they were virtually cut off otherwise.

Almost a week before their arrival, a vicious spring storm had damaged the island's radio tower and the connections to the mainland, making the phones and the two-way radios highly unreliable. Churchill had the only working satellite phone on the island, but that didn't bother Dale. Churchill had come through for him before. He'd come through again.

"Ready?" Tansy held open the door to the meeting room, and Dale hung back from the buzz of voices and motion inside. Then he sighed and nodded.

"Ready." Ready as he'd ever be.

There was a speculative murmur from the sea of tanned, weather-beaten men and women when Churchill introduced him as Dr. Metcalf. Dale bent down to the ancient microphone and did his best. *Keep the locals calm. Have a plan. Don't foster panic.* The directives spooled through his head, though in his experience with outbreaks, the rules were easier spoken than followed.

"Hi folks, and thank you all for coming. We want to keep you informed as to what's going on here. I'm Dr. Metcalf, as most of you know. Beside me is Dr. Whitmore."

The crowd quieted, save for a woman at the back of the room who sobbed into her hands. The names of the dead islanders flickered through Dale's brain and the image of the still, sheet-wrapped forms lying side by side in the temporary motel morgue settled heavily on his heart.

He continued, "Dr. Hazel is with the patients right now. We're doing everything we can for them, but we need your help. We need you to—"

"How many of us are going to die?" a red-eyed man in the front row interrupted Dale. "My Mary's already dead. Are my children going to get it? Am I?"

Your parents are gone, boy. You'll live with me.
Dale willed away the memory of Trask's voice. It had
no place here.

He gritted his teeth and answered, "There haven't
been any new cases since yesterday, and the symptoms aren't infectious. There's no reason to believe
you're in greater danger than anyone else on the island." Which wasn't entirely reassuring.

"We should leave!" shouted a woman in the back.
Curtis's mother. Her eyes were dark holes in her
head, and the deep lines beside her mouth attested to
the hours she'd spent at her son's bedside watching
him die by degrees. "We should leave Lobster Island
and never come back. This place is cursed! We lose
a dozen people a year to the sea, the catches are
worse and worse, the spring storms destroyed half the
fleet, and *now this?*" She spread her hands to the
murmuring, nodding crowd. "We should take our
families and go."

"Go where?" a beefy man in the middle of the
crowd shouted. "You said it yourself, lobstering's
been bad and half the fleet is broken beyond repair.
If we could even get the boats to the mainland, what
would we do then? Most of us are broke!"

"Broke is better than dead!" a second woman
called from the edges of the shifting, muttering sea
of islanders.

"People, people, please! I need you to calm down
and listen to me." Dale raised his hands for silence,
knowing he was on the edge of losing the crowd. "Ac-

cording to Churchill's information, the weather service is tracking a tropical depression headed this way. It should hit us in the next two or three days, which means the mainland crossing isn't safe right now."

Not that many of the shabby lobster boats would survive the crossing on a calm, clear day. The currents between Lobster Island and the Maine coast were brutal.

The buzz in the room dropped a notch, and Dale continued. "By then, we should know where the toxin is coming from, and how to fight it. Until we do, it would be best if you all continue to eat canned food and try to drink only bottled water."

There was disbelieving silence. Then a grizzled captain asked, "Where are we supposed to get bottled water?"

Dale closed his eyes. He and Tansy had raided the island's single grocery store early that morning, after spending a sleepless night helping Hazel with twenty cases of food poisoning. They'd come away from the little store with a few tins of boiled ham and a half-dozen bottles of cola.

Their downed plane had contained gallons of spring water and freeze-dried rations along with canned goods and the field kits. But until Churchill's charter arrived, they had nothing. And if the storm moved in faster than expected...

They could be in big trouble.

But the islanders didn't need to know that right now. So Dale forced a confidence he didn't feel. "Do your best. Until we know where the toxin is coming from, you shouldn't eat or drink anything that hasn't been brought in from the mainland." He leaned into the microphone. "Beyond that, if any of you experience an upset stomach, tingling or burning in your fingertips and tongue, or any other symptoms, you should come to the motel immediately. The earlier we see you, the more we can help." He hoped.

"Excuse me." A man stood up from his chair in the second row. His navy trousers, white button-down shirt and capped teeth instantly marked him as an outsider. He lifted a hand. "I'd like to say a few words."

"We know what you're gonna say, Roberts, and we don't wanna hear it," a lobster captain yelled.

A murmur of agreement bolstered this opinion, but from his seat behind Dale on the stage, Churchill called, "As acting mayor, I'll remind you that everyone in this assembly has the right to speak his or her piece. Even real estate developers."

Roberts ignored the gibe and took the podium, nudging Dale aside. "I think you'll be interested in what I have to say, especially if you wish to leave the island with enough money to start over."

Dale eased his way off the stage and headed for the door. He'd said what he'd needed to say. The islanders would need to make their own decisions now. Personally, he'd take the money and run.

Roberts continued, "I represent a group of men who are very interested in purchasing this island for development purposes."

"Yeah," shouted a whiskered man in the back, "and most of us have told you to go to hell!"

The crowd shifted and muttered, some resentful, some considering.

Dale slipped out of the room, thinking that once the outbreak was over he might talk to Roberts about selling his parents' place. HFH could use the money to replace the plane.

Tansy joined him a moment later and touched his arm. "Come on. Let's get some sleep."

Dale pulled away from her, and from the offer. "I think I'll go back to the clinic and help Hazel. I'm not that tired." It was a lie. He didn't want to go back to his parents' house. There were too many memories there. And he didn't want to be alone with Tansy. There were too many memories there, as well, and he was feeling too exposed.

"Hazel will be fine, and we both need sleep. Forty-eight hours on duty is our limit. HFH policy." She steered him to the dirt path he'd run down a thousand times in his nightmares. The path to his empty house.

It wasn't until they passed the black-shadowed hedge at the far edge of the town common that Dale saw the dark figure waiting for them, heard the faint rustle of movement, and his every sense went on instant alert.

Ambush!

Chapter Five

"Tansy, run!" He shoved her towards the brightly lit meeting house and turned to face their attacker. "Don't ask, just run!"

The shadowy figure lunged, and Dale leapt back. He stumbled over a tree root, kicked out blindly and connected, feeling a spurt of surprise when the other man went down with a grunt and didn't get up.

"Whaddid you do that for, boy?" The boozy voice rose up from the ground, and Dale's gut soured at the smell of cheap beer and cheaper gin.

He stepped back quickly and bumped into Tansy. "I told you to run," he snapped, his voice harsh with anger and embarrassment.

"I wanted to make sure you were okay," she said quietly, crouching down beside the drunk. She raised her voice. "Trask? It's Dr. Whitmore. Tansy. Can you stand?"

Leave him there, Dale wanted to say. *This is his problem, not ours.* But it saddened him to think that his uncle, a man he'd once idolized, had crawled into a bottle the day after his wife's death and still hadn't emerged, fifteen years later.

If that's what love did to a man, then Dale wanted no part of the emotion.

"Come on," Tansy said, "help me lift him up. We can't leave him here. Let's get him home."

Together, they hefted Dale's uncle to his feet and turned him towards the dusty path. Trask balked. "No. Don't wanna go home. Wanna see Hazel. My Hazel. But she won't come to the house. Says it's too much like Suzie there." His head lolled bonelessly. Dale curled his lip at the fumes and cursed the punch of pain when Trask murmured, "My Suzie."

"Let's haul him to the motel and dump him on one of the benches to sober up," Dale said roughly, hating that Tansy had seen this, hating that she knew what he'd come from. Who he might have turned into.

"Be reasonable, Dale. Hazel is busy with the patients. Let's take him home and get some coffee into him." Tansy's tone was chiding. In the darkness lit only by the reflected lights from the meeting house, her face reflected her disappointment. In him.

"Don't want to go home," Trask repeated, straightening and looking almost sober. "Need to talk to you, boy, about your parents. About Suzie. You were right—they weren't lost at sea. I've got *proof!* I've got—"

"There you are, old friend!" Churchill's voice broke into the suddenly tense moment. He and his Amazonian bodyguard-cum-chauffeur, Frankie, appeared out of the darkness. "We've been looking for you! Rumor had it you were tying one on at The Claw."

Dale winced at the thought of Churchill being forced to babysit his drunken uncle. Without a word, as though she did this five times a week, Frankie lifted Trask's limp form in a fireman's carry and walked down the dark path to the house Dale's uncle had shared with his bride.

When they were gone, Churchill touched Dale's sleeve. "If it helps any, this is the first time I've seen him drunk since the day you left." When Dale didn't answer, the older man sighed, and said, "I'm sorry you had to see this, son. I'm sorry you came back."

Then he, too, was gone, swallowed up into the shadows with only a swirl of sound to mark his passing.

Dale and Tansy were silent for a moment, then she hissed a breath. "I can't see how that would help any." She turned to him. "That man just all but accused you of driving your uncle to drink. How dare he? What right does he have?"

Anger tangled with hurt and desperation in one lonely, messy ball in Dale's chest until he snapped, "He dares because he was a friend of my parents and because he helped me escape this awful place. He has every right because he's the only one who ever gave a damn about me."

The moment the words were out, Dale wished he could call them back. But he could no more unsay the words than he could take back the shallow, self-absorbed things he'd said to his mother the night she died.

He reached out a hand in the darkness. "Tans..."

She turned away. "Never mind, Dale. It's okay. Your emotions were one of the few things you never lied about. You didn't believe I cared for you, and you sure as hell didn't care enough for me."

Dale followed her in silence up the path to his boyhood home. Part of him wished he could tell her the truth, that of all the things he'd lied about—his past, his position, his very nature—pretending not to care for her had been the biggest lie of all. And the most necessary, because he had no intention of falling in love.

Just look what it had done to his uncle.

When they reached the house, he slid the key from the pocket of his borrowed jeans and swung open the kitchen door. Tansy brushed past him without a word, but the tense set of her shoulders shouted her hurt.

Dale knew he should let her go. She was returning to the mainland the next day—whether she knew it or not—and it would be best for both of them if she hated him when she went.

But he reached out a hand towards her. "Tansy."

She halted. Turned back. "Yes, Dale?"

I'm sorry I lied about who I am. I'm sorry I didn't let you in when you asked. I'm sorry I didn't fight harder when you left. He cleared his throat. "You're in the first bedroom on the left, in my old room. Lock your window and pull the curtains, okay?"

She looked at him, and he worried, not for the first time, that she was seeing things he'd rather keep hidden. Finally, she took a breath. "What about what your uncle said? What if he has proof—"

"He has nothing," Dale interrupted. "The boat went down with all hands aboard. Period."

"But what if—"

"There is no 'what if,' Tansy." He took a deep breath, scrubbed a hand across his face and willed the headache away. Willed the heartache away. "Let's just get some sleep. We both need it."

She looked at him for a long moment before she finally turned and climbed the stairs. Dale didn't watch her go. He leaned against the bare hallway wall, closed his eyes and saw the shattered hull of an old lobster boat that had washed up on the barren southern claw, where not even the children ventured.

It had been raining when Churchill had taken him to see the wreck—big, fat drops that heralded yet another storm.

The rigging had been mostly gone and the familiar red, white and blue flag had been snapped from its pole, but there was no mistaking the name painted on her bow in crooked, childish letters. *Curly Sue.*

Standing in the rain, eye throbbing with the eggplant-colored bruise Trask had put there the day before, young Dale had clung to Churchill and cried for his parents, for the favorite aunt he'd named the boat after, and for the uncle who'd gone from hero to monster in a night.

Twelve hours later, Dale had been on a chartered plane to the mainland, with a few changes of clothes in a knapsack at his feet and a wad of cash in his pocket. He hadn't watched the shape of Lobster Island disappear in the distance.

Now, fifteen years after that, Dale pressed his fingers to his eyes and wondered, *What if?* What if he hadn't left the island? What if he'd tied Trask to a chair and poured coffee into him until he sobered up and turned back into the man Dale remembered? What if they'd investigated the *Curly Sue*'s disappearance together?

Then his thought process hit a dead end. At seventeen, he'd wanted to believe it had been something more than an accident. He'd wanted to blame someone for taking away his family. He'd convinced himself it was important that his mother never went out on the boat after dark. He'd seen evidence in the fact that his parents had said they were going for a walk that night, not a fishing run.

At thirty-two, he knew plans changed, people changed, boats sank. He'd seen the wreck himself. The *Curly Sue* had gone down in a storm, there was nothing more to it.

But a voice at the back of his head slyly insisted, *What if there* was *more? What then?*

What if he'd let his parents go unavenged for fifteen years?

UPSTAIRS IN HER BORROWED bed, Tansy finally heard the floorboards creak and held her breath, hating herself for the questions that she couldn't suppress.

What would she do if Dale knocked?

What would she do if he didn't?

His footsteps paused. Her heart thumped once. Twice. But he didn't knock. The cut-glass knob didn't turn. After a moment, the footsteps continued down the hall. A door shut in the distance.

"Damn it!" She muffled her frustrated groan in a musty pillow. "I'm hopeless."

She was no better than her mother, still wanting a man even when she *knew* he wasn't good for her. Dale liked fun times, surface relationships and cheerful women. Emotions made him uncomfortable.

Not good qualities in a husband. Or a father. And though she hadn't started out looking for such things, Tansy had changed over the two years they'd been together. Dale hadn't. At least, not until they'd reached Lobster Island.

Since then, she wasn't sure who he was. He wasn't the driven, almost obsessed field researcher she'd grown to love. He wasn't the distant, cool urban doctor of Boston General she'd grown to hate. He was someone else entirely, a native islander with a past she knew nothing about and a family he seemed not to want. And that was the most telling fact of all.

The look on his face when he'd seen his uncle lying drunk on the town common had almost broken her heart. The vulnerable mix of grief, regret and anger had touched her and made her want to soothe, but he'd made it clear he wanted nothing from her. No comfort, no emotion, and no questioning of Trask's 'proof.'

Tansy knew what it meant to lose a parent, through distance if not death. She couldn't imagine the pain of losing both mother and father at once. And then to speak of murder? It was too much.

It was clearly too much for Dale, who dealt with it like he'd so often dealt with her emotions—by closing down and ending the conversation. And for the first time, Tansy understood that for Dale, sometimes shutting down was easier than feeling.

The old pipes knocked in the bathroom, and his footsteps paced the hall again. They passed her room without faltering. Another door closed, and she imagined him slipping between the sheets.

In the field, they'd both slept fully clothed and ready for action at a moment's notice. When they were working out of their home hospital in Boston, they'd both slept naked, ready for a different sort of action. Which would he pick tonight? He was in the field, it was true.

But he was also home.

I was born here, his voice whispered in her mind as she curled up beneath the bedspread, fully clothed.

Images jostled her mind, from the plane crash nearly forty-eight hours earlier to the sight of a small boy lying in a cheap motel bed, hooked to a respirator. A faceless shadow leered at her through shower steam, and Dale's remembered touch seared her flesh with a heat that was akin to pain.

Though her body begged for sleep, ached for it,

her mind raced in overdrive, revving along at speeds unimagined even by the plane that had sunk in Lobster Bay.

"Go. To. Sleep," she whispered fiercely, but her eyes popped open and she stared out into the darkness. There were no streetlights, but the slim crescent moon provided enough light to pick out the silhouette of a lone photograph. She had noticed it when she'd entered the room and debated slamming the door. In it, a towheaded boy in a navy knit cap stood proudly beside an older, taller version of himself. A small, light-haired beauty had completed the family picture.

Though most of the furnishings in the room bore traces of long neglect and a recent dusting, the photograph, or at least the frame, looked brand new.

Tansy stared at the dark oval, wondering who'd put it there. Mickey? Trask? And why? To welcome Dale home? To remind him? Chastise him?

She yawned. And why, she thought as she tumbled toward sleep through a dizzying maze of images, did she care so much? They were on the island to solve an outbreak. Nothing more. Dale wasn't her problem anymore, he'd made that painfully clear, time and time again.

On that thought, she slid sideways into a warm dream...

LOBSTERS SCUTTLED BETWEEN her feet. When she cringed and shrank away, one level of her mind registered the hot, sweaty sheets tangling her legs. The intimate touch made her think of Dale.

She stretched sinuously on the bed, inviting him, rejecting him, feeling his hands burn her flesh wherever they touched. Just like it had always been between them.

"Oh, Dale," she breathed. "Yes." And the air backed up in her lungs. She thought she might never breathe again. Then she did.

And it burned.

"God!" Tansy jerked awake and sat up, clawing at the smothering darkness that wasn't dark anymore but rather pulsed red-orange.

The air above the bed clogged her lungs. She coughed and her heart jackrabbited. *Smoke!* It seared her lungs and raked at her nose and throat when she tried to scream.

Only a thin mewling emerged into the foul, thick air, and the small sound was instantly swallowed up by the roar of the beast that surrounded her.

Fire!

A CRACKLING NOISE AND THE thump of footsteps woke Dale from a shallow, restless sleep. "What the—" His half-formed question dissolved in a fit of coughing and he lunged for the floor, instincts taking over before his brain caught up.

Fire! he thought in a quick moment of sleep-dulled panic, then *Tansy!*

His dream had been so strong, so real, that he

reached for the bed before remembering she wasn't there. They weren't together anymore. She was down the hall. In danger.

"Tansy!" he yelled over the serpent's hiss of smoke and the lion's roar of fire beneath. God, the whole place must've gone up. Footsteps. He'd heard footsteps. Maybe Tansy was already safe.

Or maybe she was in even greater danger. Dale would have cursed himself, but he couldn't waste the breath.

Something crashed downstairs and the floor beneath him shook. Shuddered. Swayed. For an instant, he flashed back to huddling with Tansy in a crude doorway as aftershocks ripped through a broken village and sent ruined huts tumbling together. Then he was on his feet, ducking low and running for the door. He prayed the floor was still strong enough to hold him.

It should have been dark in the hallway, but the very air glowed with an eerie orange light. The crackle of flames downstairs brought the image of a ski lodge fireplace gone mad, and the acrid smoke burning his nostrils reminded him of the dead and the dying he'd once helped pull from a torched nightclub.

"Tansy? Are you in there?" he yelled towards his old bedroom. Something told him she was, told him those hadn't been her footsteps in the hall. "I'm coming in. Get back from the door," he shouted, hoping she could hear him. Hoping he wasn't too late.

There was no response over the rush of dry, burning wood and the voice of the fire. He ducked below the waist-high smoke and gulped a breath before testing the knob to his boyhood room. It was cool in comparison to the foul, blazing air that surrounded him, and he breathed a prayer as he yanked open the door and bolted inside the small room.

"Tansy? Where are you?" The space was filled with dry, hot smoke. Through watering eyes and the eerie red radiance that bathed the entire house, he saw that the bed was empty, and his heart stuttered.

Then he saw Tansy. She was lying on the floor in mid-crawl. Out cold.

He dropped to his hands and knees, trying to find fresh air while he checked her vitals. She was breathing, thank God, and stirred feebly when he shook her. "Come on, babe. We're out of here."

Half carrying, half dragging her, Dale got them both into the hallway, coughing and trying to stay low. The roar was deafening, and the heat drove him back two paces before his slitted eyes registered the sight before him.

The stairway was an inferno.

"Is there—" Tansy coughed against his shoulder and hid her face. Tears made sooty tracks down her cheeks, looking like blood in the red firelight. "Is there another way down?"

"No. Just the stairs." Heart pounding, fear drumming at his temples, Dale looked down into the yellow-black vortex that had once been the front hall. How long until the stairs collapsed? How long until the whole damn place came down around them? He sucked in a smoky breath and fought the urge to retch. Outside, he could just make out frantic shouts and the blare of the air horn mounted on the island's only water truck.

Too little, too late. They'd be better served by hosing down the trees near the house to keep the fire from spreading.

The tree!

"Come on!" he yelled. "Over here!" He pulled Tansy across the hallway and into the ancient bathroom, slamming the door behind them.

The smoke was thinner there, filtering out through the open bathroom window. Dale waved toward the tree. "Out you go! One foot goes on the gutter there, reach your other leg out for that big branch, jump and grab on, okay?"

The unearthly brightness of the fire surrounded them, making the outside world seem darker and colder than inside the little room. But Tansy, never flinched. She looked up at him, pupils huge in the flickering light. Unable to resist, he leaned down and kissed her, hard.

The flare of heat could be blamed on the flames surrounding them, but the desperate kick of his heart was Tansy. Only Tansy.

Shaken, afraid, Dale pulled back and shoved her toward the window. "Go! Get the hell out of here!"

And then she was gone, into the darkness, leaving him in the flames.

There was a shattering crash from the front of the house, and the whole structure trembled. Dale could swear the tiles beneath his feet swayed. Or maybe it was the smoke getting to him. With Tansy safely away, it was suddenly harder to breathe. The heat didn't seem so bad anymore. In fact, he thought it might be nice to sit on the floor for a moment before he attempted the climb down. He was tired. So tired.

His knees buckled.

"Don't you dare, Dale Metcalf," Tansy yelled through the open window. Damn her, she was still in the tree!

He struggled to his feet, wheezing. "Tansy, get down from there right now!"

"Just as soon as you get out here with me," she countered. Her eyes were wide and scared. Her mouth worked when another crash sounded from the front of the house and a few of the nearest branches burst into flame. "Come on. Just like you told me. One foot on the gutter, the other on the branch. Come on, I'll catch you."

The simple knowledge that she wasn't leaving without him was enough to propel Dale across the room and out the window.

Where he discovered the gutter was gone.

"Just jump and grab!" Tansy screamed. "There's no time. Jump and grab!"

Flames detonated through the bathroom door with a sound like a nuclear explosion, and Dale jumped. He caught a midsized branch with one hand, a knot-hole with a toe. He teetered for a moment, flailed with his free arm.

And felt a delicate hand close over his wrist.

"I've got you," she yelled. "Hang on!"

Together, they worked their way down the tree that had provided him an escape from the dreary boredom of homework so many nights in the distant past, when he'd gone down to the water, watched the stars and dreamed of being a lobster captain like his father. And his uncle.

"Are you okay? Damn, your pa's house burnt down!" A lobsterman in a firefighter's hat pulled them away from the house just as the tanker truck began spraying seawater across the hellish inferno. "There's nobody else inside, is there?"

"No," Dale replied between coughs, bracing Tansy as she clung. But he thought, *Not unless the bastard who torched the place is still in there.*

"Did you leave the bathroom window open?" Tansy asked, her voice rough and raw.

He shook his head. "No. And I heard footsteps." Needing the contact and the reassurance, even though he didn't deserve it after dragging her to this awful place, Dale hugged Tansy and breathed in the smoke that clung to her hair. He felt her arms creep around his waist and closed his eyes.

He had to get her out of here. She'd be safe on the mainland.

"Dale! Tansy! Are you okay?" Hazel arrived at a dead run with a portable first-aid kit slung over her shoulder. Behind her, the island's entire population gathered in shifting, murmuring knots of people.

Hazel reached for them, her eyes going to the house, which was engulfed in flames. "God! What happened?"

At the stark terror in her expression, Dale felt something shift in his chest. He'd been gone for a long time, but some connections seemed to have survived whether he wanted them to or not.

"We made it out," he assured her. He rubbed a hand along Tansy's arm and repeated, "We got out."

He glanced back at the house. It hurt to look at it, both because the yellow flames had burned through and were shooting brightly into the sky, and because it just *hurt,* somewhere deep inside him. The old house had withstood his parents' deaths and his escape from Lobster Island, but it hadn't survived his return. Or an arsonist who didn't want him back.

But who? And why? Was it because of the outbreak, or because of past history?

Tansy shivered and he tightened his arms around her, drawing as much comfort as he gave. He could have been killed. *She* could have been killed. And she was worth two of him.

"I'm sorry I got you into this," he murmured into her hair, wishing he had the guts to take the risk that caring brought. But he didn't. Instead, he promised, "We'll get you off the island tomorrow."

"The hell you will!" She jabbed an elbow into his ribs and spun to face him. "I'm not leaving here without you. Got that, Metcalf? I didn't desert you in Tehru, and I'm not going to leave you now."

Worry shifted to anger born of fear. She had to leave. He couldn't be responsible for what would happen if she stayed.

"There's a big difference between the two situations, Tansy." He kept his voice calm, knowing coldness would annoy her more than a shout. "We were lovers in Tehru. Don't think that just because I kissed you in there, it means I want you back. Don't you get it? I don't want you here."

The lie stuck between his teeth, so much more difficult than the casual falsities that had defined his life for so long now. It was different because *this* was different.

This was Tansy.

Temper hissed from her lips, but before she could reply, Hazel stepped in. "Well, you two seem unharmed, at the very least. I'll be getting back to the motel then. Eddie isn't doing well. His kidneys are struggling."

To Dale, the reminder was a colder dose of reality than the salty spray coming from the tanker truck. There were sick people on the island, and it was his job to keep them alive and figure out what was making them sick. He could do it alone. He *had* to do it alone. So he nodded. "We'll come with you. We've slept long enough."

He'd keep Tansy close to his side until the plane came to take her away. Anyone who wanted to get to her would have to go through him first.

"Nonsense." Walter Churchill stepped from the shadows, making Dale wonder how long he'd been there. "You'll both come home with me. You should have stayed at my house in the first place. Your parents' house was drier than a pile of kindling and the wiring was older than me. It was an accident waiting to happen."

Dale shrugged, but didn't mention the footsteps he'd heard. That information would stay between him and Tansy. For now. As soon as she was gone, the investigation could begin in earnest.

"Churchill is right," Hazel agreed. "You're both exhausted, and probably in shock. Go clean yourselves up and sleep at the mansion. I'll see you in the morning." She shooed them in the direction of Churchill's dark SUV, which was parked beside the now empty tanker truck. "We'll trade shifts then."

Tansy balked. "But if Eddie needs us—"

"Eddie needs a miracle," Hazel replied flatly. "He's not clearing the toxin out of his system. If he doesn't wake up in the next twelve hours or so, I don't think he's going to make it."

Dale flinched. He'd thought the same, but hearing it out loud made it real. "There has to be *something* we can do," he grated, aware of a fragmentary thought that hovered just out of reach. Something about another island? He wasn't sure. But the memory smelled like rum and baked desserts.

That, or the smoke had gotten to him.

"Come on," Tansy whispered, tugging at his arm.

"She's right. Let's go with Churchill and get some sleep."

But still he hung back. It wasn't that he wanted to stay and watch his boyhood home smolder. It wasn't that he really felt his presence mattered to Eddie one way or the other. It was...

The thought fled and Dale ground his teeth in frustration. He wasn't sure what it was. Tansy was right. He needed some downtime, or he'd be no use to her or the patients. "Okay. We'll crash at Walter's."

Besides, he needed to talk to Churchill about the plane. He wanted it here fast, and he wanted Tansy on it.

As the black SUV backed down the vehicle-choked driveway, there was a splintering crash from the burning house. Dale turned back in time to see the tree list sideways and fall. Roots silhouetted against a bloodred pile of coals, the old friend that had saved his life died a fiery death and lay still.

He turned his face away and heard Churchill murmur, "Drive on, Frankie."

Yes, thought Dale. *Drive on and keep driving. Maybe we can reach the mainland by morning.*

At least there, Tansy would be safe.

Chapter Six

In Churchill's guest quarters an hour later, Tansy should have felt pampered and relaxed as she floated in the waist-deep bath. The water was scented with rose oil, a hundred tiny jets feathered across her body and a new robe lay neatly folded beside a pile of thick towels. But she was tense and teary. Her throat stung, her eyes hurt...

And someone had tried to kill her and Dale.

What the hell had they gotten themselves into? She was beginning to think she should have swum home the moment she discovered Dale's history on Lobster Island.

"Yeah, right." She scrubbed at a soot stain on her arm, avoiding the raw, burned patch beside it. "Like you'd leave him here alone. Face it, you're hopeless when it comes to Dale Metcalf."

"I'm sorry. I didn't mean to eavesdrop on your conversation with...yourself."

She swallowed a gasp and twisted toward the sound of his voice, lifting her hands to shield her bare breasts. "Damn it, Dale! What are you doing here?"

He was leaning against the elaborately carved doorframe, wearing a masculine robe that gaped open at the chest and thigh. His smoke-reddened eyes were intent, though the emotions behind them were cloaked. "I thought I'd use the bath, but it seems otherwise occupied."

The water, which had been comfortably warm moments before, suddenly sizzled around her. How many times had they played out this same scene in the past? Bathrooms had always been a favorite play place for them. It was symbolic, she supposed, an antithesis of the filth, sickness and desperation of their normal assignments. In this way, they came to each other clean. Or at least they used to.

She swallowed hard, found her voice and willed it to stay steady when she said, "I'm sure you have a bath in your own guest suite. I recall Walter saying it was down the hall."

"Not anymore. I told him we'd share."

She shot to her feet. "What?" Ignoring his raised eyebrows and her nudity, she climbed out of the bath and stalked over to her robe, yanked it on. "What do you mean, you told him we'd share? What happened to 'I don't want you here'? Damn it, Dale. What sort of a game are you playing?"

He didn't move, but his eyes flared, reminding her that she didn't know Dale Metcalf as well as she'd once thought. Didn't know what he was capable of.

The idea was a little thrilling and more than a bit frightening.

But why was he insisting they stay together? Before, it had seemed that he couldn't get away from her fast enough.

Tansy walked over to him and poked him in the chest. Her finger speared through the loosened flaps of his robe and glanced off hard flesh, right above the lobster tattoo. She ignored the low buzz of her blood and demanded, "Why the sudden need for togetherness? What do you know that I don't?"

He caught her hand and held it hard, and the warmth of his skin reminded her of their earlier kiss. "Someone tried to kill us tonight. I don't know who it was, or why. Until I do, I'm not letting you out of my sight. Got it?"

Though the harsh possessiveness of his tone called to something deep within her, Tansy held herself away from temptation and fired back, "We're perfectly safe here. Didn't you see the security system? And the..." The look in his eye stalled her. "You don't think Walter has anything to do with this, do you? What possible reason would he have to want us dead? He was your parents' friend!"

Dale shook his head and cursed. "No. I don't think it's Churchill. I don't know what to think, if you want the honest truth. But I know I'm tired and I won't sleep unless I know you're safe, so be a pal, okay, Tansy? Let me stay here."

Be a pal. The words were sexless, and because of

it, they stung. Tansy grimaced. "A pal, sure. We'll just share a bed, nothing to it. We're both grown-ups, right?"

Grown-ups and ex-lovers. But if he could ignore the pull of the past, and the brief, desperate flare they'd felt during the fire, so could she. Besides, he was right. They were in danger, and better off together than apart.

There was a short daybed beside the airy window, and enough blankets and fluffy pillows to make a nest four times the size of their pallet in Tehru. But by unspoken accord, they walked to the big bed together. The clothes Mickey had lent them were smoky and torn beyond repair. Churchill had promised replacements in the morning. Until then, it was robes or nothing.

They both kept their robes on.

"You still sleep on the left?" he asked politely.

Tansy smothered a snort. "Dale, it's only been three months. You think I've changed that much?" She slid beneath the covers and stayed close to the left edge of the springy mattress.

He turned out the last light and she felt the bed dip beneath his weight. "I don't know," he answered, finally. "It seems like a lot longer. I guess I figured that maybe you'd found another…arrangement you liked better."

He was right. The months had felt like years, for many reasons. Tears crowded Tansy's eyes when she replied, "No, Dale. No other arrangements. Nothing's changed."

He didn't answer for so long she thought he'd fallen asleep. Then he sighed and said, "Yeah. Nothing's changed." The mattress swayed as he rolled over, facing away from her. "Try to get some rest, okay? In the morning, we'll figure out how to get you home."

Too tired to argue about it, Tansy merely murmured, "'Night," and closed her eyes. Though she was still shaky from the fire, and her throat hurt like hell, she drifted off quickly, warmed by the man at her back and the stealthy feeling of safety that snuck up on her when she was in that vulnerable place between asleep and awake.

SHE DREAMED OF TEHRU, of the bombs and the screams, and of the love that she'd found there, in the ugliest place on earth. Strange, that she'd found something so beautiful amid so much awfulness. She dreamed of the weekend she and Dale had taken for themselves later that year, on the way home from yet another disaster area.

The shabby old hotel in the Philippines had once been glorious, but the architecture had held little fascination. They'd been content to stay in bed for forty-eight hours of no responsibility except to each other. Leave, the HFH head honchos had called it, but by the end of the weekend, it had felt more like love.

Tangled together, not sure where one left off and the other began, they'd eaten little and slept even less, always waking to reach for each other once more. He would prop himself on one elbow and gaze down at her with those glorious blue eyes. She would reach up and trace a finger along his dear, stubbled cheek. In that last moment before their lips touched, their breaths would mingle and become one. Their hearts would beat in tandem, and—

And this was no dream, Tansy realized. Her eyes fluttered open, registering the gray light of pre-dawn and the shadow of a man above her. Then he closed the distance between them, or she did. It didn't matter, because in the next instant their lips touched and all rational thought fled.

Never familiar, always new and potent, Dale's flavor slid across her tongue like an old friend and Tansy, half-awake and needy after so many months, arched into the contact. The kiss deepened immediately, like a continued conversation without beginning or end, existing only in the now.

She opened to him with a murmur, not knowing whether he was awake and not caring, only grateful, so grateful to taste him again. To feel him wrap around her and draw her in, to the one place where she felt safe. And warm. So warm.

He smelled of smoke, or maybe she did, and she pressed closer to him beneath the fine sheets, feeling the robe bunch behind her, leaving her legs bare to tangle with his.

The rough hair against her skin was shocking. It chased the last of the sleep from Tansy's brain, which fired an urgent message of *Wrong!* This was wrong. She started to pull away just as Dale jerked back.

"Damn!" He leapt off the bed and stood, tugging his robe closed, though not before she glimpsed the hard, jutting flesh that had once been hers for the taking. "I'm sorry."

Tansy closed her eyes against the sight and the memory. A hot blush flooded her face, and she was glad he couldn't see it in the gray half light. "I'm sorry, too. I was…sleeping." Dreaming. Wishing. "I didn't mean it."

When had lying become easy?

"Yeah." Dale cleared his throat and took another step away from the bed. "Me neither. Sorry." He pulled a blanket off the daybed, snagged a pillow and tossed them both on the floor. "I guess sharing the bed was a bad idea."

"Guess so." Tansy rolled onto her side so she wouldn't have to watch him wrap himself in the blanket and stretch out on the floor. Tears stung her eyes. She was too proud to let them fall, though her pride was growing brittle and thin.

A tear broke free. Impatiently, she scrubbed at it with the corner of the sheet. The absence of the other pillow echoed hollowly against her back, making the empty side of the bed feel lonelier than it had in the past three months.

"Tans?" His voice rose from the floor, accompanied by a rustle of movement. "I really am sorry. I shouldn't have kissed you like that."

I shouldn't have kissed you at all, was the unspoken meaning. It galled her that he had so easily walked away from what they'd had together. Then again, that just went to show how one-sided their relationship had been. She'd been hurt. He hadn't.

She swiped at her face again, then willed her voice not to tremble when she answered, "It was my fault. I was dreaming about the Philippines."

There was a long pause, and she felt even stupider than before. There was nothing more pitiful than admitting she'd been dreaming about him. And since they hadn't done anything *besides* make love on the island, he'd instantly know what she had been—

"That's it!" Dale surged up from the floor, a strange, robed figure with wild eyes. "You've got it!"

Her traitorous heart sped to match his excitement and she sat up. "What? Dale, what is it?"

"The Philippines! Tansy, you're a genius." He strode to the door, opened it and called down the hall, "Frankie? Churchill? We need those clothes, stat. We've got to get to the general store, then over to the motel."

"Dale," she snapped, confusion and excitement battling within her, "what the hell are you talking about?"

He stopped in the middle of the room, a figure of sculpted beauty in a terry cloth robe. He lifted both hands as if to say, *It's so simple*. His smile reminded her of the day they'd found the source of the Tehruvian outbreak, a villager who'd been selling turtles caught in an infected pond. He said, "The Philippines, Tans. Coconut and brown sugar."

She felt the jolt all the way down to her toes. But it wasn't a sexual jolt this time. It was a lightning bolt of understanding.

Coconut and brown sugar. It was the Philippines' native cure for paralytic shellfish poisoning.

"YOU SURE THIS'LL WORK?" Churchill eyed the packages in Dale's lap as the SUV bumped towards the motel.

"It'll work." It had to, or Eddie wasn't going to make it, Dale thought as they pulled into the motel parking lot. The boy's body wasn't clearing the toxin fast enough, and his other systems were failing.

Then Dale's thoughts stuttered to a halt and his doctor's focus shattered at the sight of Mickey sitting outside the motel room with his wife cradled against his chest.

Oh, God. They were too late.

He was out of the SUV before it stopped rolling, and across the parking lot in three long strides. "Mickey, I'm so—"

"Shh." Dale's cousin lifted a finger to his lips. "Libby's finally sleeping. It's been days." Then, apparently seeing Dale's panic, Mickey smiled sadly. "No, Dale. There's been no change. Our Eddie's still…waiting." He sighed and shifted his wife in his arms. "And so are we."

When Mickey touched his lips to Libby's temple, where her wheat-blond hair gave way to pale skin, Dale felt something shift inside his chest. Family.

That's what Trask had taken away from him. Family, and love. Why hadn't he seen it before?

Or had he seen it and just not cared?

"You ready to try this?" Tansy touched his hand, and it was all Dale could do not to reach for her, to take from her the same comfort Mickey was sharing with his Libby.

He could still taste Tansy on his lips, still feel her beneath him. She'd been dreaming of the Philippines. Well, he'd been wide-awake and had known exactly what he was doing.

And still hadn't been able to stop himself. Tansy was his weakness, an aching, poignant reminder of everything he'd lost.

Everything he couldn't afford.

"Try what?" Mick whispered. His faded blue eyes lit on the package in Tansy's arms. "Do you have a cure for Eddie?"

Dale willed away the memory of Tansy rising up from Churchill's guest bath like a mermaid emerging from the sea. Focus. He had to focus on the patients.

And the fact that someone wanted him and Tansy dead.

"We have something that might help," Tansy answered. "Maybe."

She shifted the package in her arms and Dale thought of the few things they'd found on the shelves of the unlocked general store. He wasn't sure a five-pound bag of shaved, processed coconut and a six-pack of expired coconut milk would have the same effect as the fresh stuff the islanders used, but it would have to do. He was just grateful the store had stocked that much, along with three boxes of dark brown sugar.

It was a relatively untested cure, but a single journal article had claimed the islanders' remedy helped buffer the patient's liver and kidneys from shellfish toxins, and helped the body clear the poisons.

Besides, Eddie and the others would die if they didn't do something soon. So Dale found a reassuring smile, dropped a hand on his cousin's shoulder and squeezed. "We'll try our best, Mick."

"Come on," Tansy urged him, "let's do this."

Even before they pushed open the door to Eddie's room, they heard the raised voices. Dale instantly recognized Hazel's normally calm tones being overridden by a familiar bellow. He shouldered his way into the room, coconut and brown sugar forgotten on a surge of anger.

"Leave her alone, Trask." Blood roaring in his ears, Dale took a menacing step towards his uncle before belatedly realizing something other than violence was thrumming through the room. He didn't need Tansy's touch on his arm to suggest he back down. The snap of temper in Hazel's eyes and the dull red flush climbing his uncle's neck was enough to drive Dale back a step. "I…uh—"

"We've brought something for Eddie." Tansy calmly stepped into the room. "It's a homeopathic remedy for PSP, but there's evidence that it works."

"Thank God. If we don't do something for him soon…" Hazel glanced down at the boy in the bed. He seemed smaller than he had before, as though the toxin was sucking him dry, ounce by ounce. Then she looked from Dale to Trask and back. Her lips firmed with decision. "Tansy and I will deal with this. Dale, I want you to go with your uncle."

"I'm not leaving Tansy," he said quickly. She would only be on the island a few more hours. He planned on sticking with her until then, keeping her safe from the faceless enemy that wanted them dead.

And once she was gone? He'd face the questions alone, as it was meant to be.

"Mickey is outside to keep watch, and it's almost daylight. We're safe." Hazel's voice hardened. "Go with Trask. You owe it to Kristin and Thomas to see what he's found."

Kristin. Thomas. Dale hadn't consciously thought of his parents' names in many years, but there they were, hovering at the edges of his mind. Along with the words *I think your parents were murdered* and *I have proof.*

Dale looked at Trask, saw that his eyes were clear of drink, though bloodshot from the night before. For a moment, it seemed that he could see the hero he'd once loved in the face of the man Trask had become.

Tansy touched Dale's shoulder before she moved to the boy's bedside. "I'll be okay with Hazel. We'll take care of Eddie and the others. You go ahead."

A part of him was surprised by Tansy's urging. He'd expected her to be put off by his roots, and to be ashamed of his drunken uncle and the questions surrounding his parents' deaths. By the fact that he'd run rather than stand up for them.

Or maybe, Dale thought as he watched Tansy brush a wisp of hair from Eddie's brow, maybe he'd been wrong all along.

Maybe *he* was the one that was ashamed.

He looked from Trask to Hazel and back again, conscious of the way the two stood shoulder-to-shoulder, united against him. Or maybe for him. Finally, he nodded. "Okay. Show me your 'proof.'"

"I have something else you'll need to see first," Trask grunted, laconic even in victory. He turned away and strode out the door to the parking lot.

Before he followed, Dale crossed to Tansy and briefly touched her cheek with the back of his hand. "I'll be back as soon as I can. Be careful."

She nodded but didn't speak, and the wariness at the back of her eyes tore at him. He knew he was sending mixed signals, but he couldn't help himself. The danger to her was breaking through the layers of self-defense and laying him bare. He wanted her, but he didn't want to need her. In caring lay pain.

He stepped away and repeated, "Be careful."

Outside, he glanced at the sky. Clouds were gathering above the island, and a low, sullen sky glow-

ered from the west, cutting them off from the mainland. A dank-smelling breeze touched his face.

The storm was coming. And it was going to be a
bad one.

WHEN DALE WAS GONE, TANSY felt his absence like
an ache. Or maybe that was the rawness from the
burned places and the bruises from the airplane crash.
She couldn't even tell anymore. She was in the midst
of the Mad Hatter's tea party and wasn't sure where
she was supposed to sit anymore.

Patients were dying. Someone had tried to kill her
and Dale. Someone, it seemed, might have killed his
parents a long time ago. Was it the same someone?
Who knew?

Certainly not Tansy. She knew nothing. *Knowledge is power.* She had no power here.

What sort of a place was this Lobster Island? What
sort of a man grew up here, then spent half his life
trying to pretend he hadn't?

"Come on. Help me with this stomach tube."
Hazel stood beside Eddie's bed holding a bottle filled
with a slurry of coconut and brown sugar. "Then
we'll sit and wait."

"And pray," Tansy added. Pray for the little boy,
and for Mickey and Libby, who were sitting outside
holding hands. Pray for Dale, who was looking more
anguished each moment, though he hid those emotions almost as well as he hid all the others. Pray for
their safety against the faceless danger that seemed

to have targeted two doctors who only wanted to help. And pray for an island that was sick at its soul, an island that saw more deaths than it should, and would see hunger come wintertime.

"Yes, pray," Hazel agreed. The women worked together to dose the little boy. Though neither mentioned it, both were hoping for an instant recovery, for Eddie's eyes to open and his mouth to turn up in a smile. But of course that didn't happen. The respirator continued its *whoosh-chug,* and little Eddie didn't move. Not even his eyelids flickered.

"Damn it," Tansy murmured after a moment. "Just damn it."

"It's too soon. Give it time to work." Hazel handed her an alcohol-soaked wipe. "Let's clean up the mess and dose the other patients. He'll be back for you soon."

"I wasn't thinking about Dale," Tansy answered too quickly, then turned away on the pretext of wiping up a spot of sugar.

After a moment, Hazel said, "You're good for him, you know."

Tansy's throat closed and the words backed up in her chest. No, she wasn't good for him. Wasn't good enough for him. Just wasn't enough.

When there was no reply, Hazel continued, "He wrote to Mickey, maybe once or twice a year, and Mick passed the letters around. The last few mentioned you."

"Oh." Tansy told herself it shouldn't still hurt after all these months. She'd had plenty of practice telling her colleagues about the breakup, since Dale hadn't told anyone. He'd pretended as though the affair had never happened. Had never ended. And that had hurt just as much as it tore at Tansy now to say, "We broke up. Three months ago."

She dropped her wipe and crossed to stand by the window, staring out at the ugly parking lot.

Hazel's touch on her shoulder was gentle. "He'd never mentioned a woman in his letters before. Not once in fifteen years."

Tansy closed her eyes, telling herself it meant nothing. "We're too different. He won't let me in."

"He's just like his uncle, then."

She turned at the flatness in the older woman's voice. Hazel fiddled with the respirator, though it needed no adjustment.

And in that moment, Tansy realized she wasn't alone. For the first time in a long, long while, someone else understood what she was going through. What she was feeling. "Trask mentioned you last night." She wasn't sure if the knowledge would help or hurt. "When he was…"

"Drunk," Hazel finished for her. She frowned. "That was a surprise, as he hasn't touched a drop in fifteen years. When Dale left, Trask realized what he'd done, what he'd become, and he stopped drinking." She blew out a frustrated breath. "But he never got past what happened. Maybe it's the island. Maybe the tragedy. I don't know. But whatever it was, it left him closed off. Hard. He'll let me into his bed, into his life, but only so far." Her lips thinned. "Sometimes, I hate him for it."

Sex without deep emotion. Love without its return. Tansy winced, knowing she could so easily fall into Hazel's role. Her mother's role.

But would it truly be worse than the loneliness of the past three months?

Wishing she didn't still care, she said, "Tell me about it. Dale's parents died?"

"And Trask's wife. Sue." There was a complex layer of feeling in Hazel's voice when she said the other woman's name. Regret. Compassion.

Resentment.

"What happened to them? Why does Trask think they were—"

A noise from the doorway interrupted her, and Dale's voice finished the question with a single word.

"Murdered."

Tansy turned to find him standing just inside the room, filling it with the punch of power that she always felt when he was near. He shook his head. "I don't know yet." He gestured out to the parking lot, where Mickey's jeep sat waiting. "I need to show you something on the airstrip. Then we'll go to Trask's house together."

Together. Though she'd often longed for the word, Tansy's heart chilled at their destination, and at the dangerous calm on Dale's face that usually meant he was hiding some deep, unwanted emotion.

Like fear.

She traded glances with Hazel, then nodded. "Of course. Let's go." He didn't touch her as they walked to the jeep, but she noticed he stayed close. Very close.

They bumped along the rutted tracks in a silence broken only by the squeak of worn axles and corroded springs. When they reached the airfield, they drove across the parking lot and turned down the runway itself. A quarter mile from the end, Tansy saw a spray of wiring and insulation, a few bolts and the beginnings of a silver scar in the tarmac. Icy fear sliced through her, along with the memory of those last few moments on the runway.

The scrape extended all the way to the end of the island, where a few broken trees leaned drunkenly against each other.

She shuddered, remembering the feeling of the plane slewing wildly, out of control. Falling...

"What the hell is he doing here?" Dale muttered, snapping her from her memories. He wheeled the jeep in beside Churchill's familiar black SUV and jumped out, leaving her to climb from the vehicle at her own pace. It was just as well. Seeing the crash site had affected her more than she'd expected. She needed a few moments to brace her wobbly legs before she joined the men, who were standing to the side of the runway, amidst the sawgrass.

She walked over to them and stopped dead when she saw the silver glint on the ground. "Oh, God."

Coiled snakelike, the airplane cable lay waiting,

frayed at one end where the force of the plane had snapped the trip wire.

But not before it had sheared off the landing gear.

Tansy's knees gave out and she was barely aware of Dale's strong arms holding her up, or of the warmth of his body against hers. Here was the final, irrefutable proof. Someone had tried to kill her and Dale. Worse, they'd come back afterwards to coil the cable, yet they hadn't taken it with them. To her, that spoke of stupidity.

Or worse, arrogance.

Churchill cursed under his breath. "Trask told me about it just now, but seeing it…makes it worse." He ran a hand through his neatly-trimmed silver hair and glanced at Dale. "And I have bad news."

What could be worse than this? Tansy thought. Then, realizing she was clinging to Dale like a helpless, hysterical female, she shoved away and stood on her own. But even gripping her hands tightly together couldn't stop the trembles. She forced her voice level and said, "I want to go home, Dale." When both men turned toward her, she lifted her chin. "We should return to Boston and regroup. We can come back in a few days with more manpower, and the authorities." This was beyond the scope of HFH.

Beyond their control.

"There's a plane coming today to take you home," Dale said quietly. But before Tansy could challenge him on the "you" part of the statement, Churchill shook his head.

"That's the bad news, I'm afraid. No plane." When Dale spun and snarled, the older man spread his soft-looking hands. "The storm—which is now officially Hurricane Harriet—is moving faster than they originally thought it would. She's headed straight up the coast, and we'll feel the first wind and waves later today." He grimaced. "Sorry. No plane until after the storm passes. Until then…"

Tansy closed her eyes and let the knowledge rattle through her. When Dale touched her shoulder, she didn't move away.

He voiced her thoughts aloud. "Until then, we're trapped on an island with an uncontained outbreak, minimal safe food and water, and someone trying to kill us."

When Tansy opened her eyes, she saw a look of determination cross Churchill's face. "You'll be safe with me, Dale. We can batten down the mansion and ride out the storm together." When Dale hesitated, Churchill stuck out his hand. "You can trust me. Have I ever let you down before?"

After a long moment, Dale shook on it. "No, Churchill. You've never let me down before."

Tansy hoped like hell he wouldn't start now.

Chapter Seven

When they reached Trask's house on the outskirts of town, Dale parked the jeep and glanced over at Tansy's grim expression. The sight of the wire had scared her. Hell, it had unnerved him, too. Even before they'd reached the island, someone had decided to kill them.

Even so, this silent Tansy worried him. He was used to seeing her fight, not withdraw.

After a moment, he cleared his throat. "Churchill is right. We can hide in the mansion until the weather clears and backup arrives. You'll be safe there, I promise."

Her breath hissed out suddenly, and she turned on him, eyes alight with frustration. "Maybe I'll be safe, but what about the patients, Dale?" Her chin jutted out in a familiar, stubborn expression. "What about your parents?"

Oddly enough, the expected anger didn't soothe him—it ticked him off. Hadn't she figured out yet that she was in *danger?* His temper spiked, and

where before he'd been able to counter her hot temper with cold control, now Dale felt his command
slip. His voice rose. "This isn't about the patients or
my parents, Tansy. This is about keeping you alive.
Or had you forgotten that someone has tried to kill
you? Twice?"

Tansy fired back, "This *is* about the patients, Dale.
We can't help them if we're hiding in Churchill's
house. And it sure as hell *is* about your parents, unless
there's another reason someone would want you dead."

"Those are my problems, not yours." She was
right, but Dale didn't want her anywhere near the
questions he'd been asking himself. What had happened that night fifteen years ago on the *Curly Sue*?
Why hadn't any of the bodies washed up with the
wreckage? And why had his parents and his aunt
gone out on the boat when they said they were going
for a walk?

They were old questions. Unanswered questions.

She sighed and the corners of her mouth turned
down. "The patients are my problem because I'm an
HFH doctor, Dale. You can't take that away from
me." She glanced over at him. "And as for the other,
I'm making it my problem because I loved you, once.
You can't take that away from me, either."

Loved. Past tense. And though she had never said
the word to him before, Dale had known it was there.

And now he knew it was gone. Funny, he
would've expected to feel relieved that she was ready
to give up on them. Instead, he felt hollow.

He glanced over and saw the shadows in her eyes. Her bravado was a thin mask covering the worry. He wished he could pull her across the vehicle, into his arms, and never let her go. But the time for that, like her love, was past. So he scowled at the gathering clouds instead.

"Let's see what Trask has to say," he finally said, unclipping his seat belt and opening the door. "I've kept him waiting long enough."

Dale took Tansy's hand to help her over the threshold, or maybe to steady himself. He cursed when he saw the same old ratty red sofa, faded now to pink. His eyes glanced over the same afghan, made by his mother's mother, and the same cabbage rose tea service, brought home by his great-grandfather after World War I.

"Nothing's changed," he grumbled softly. "Why hasn't anything changed?"

The air still smelled of citrus from the bitter orange soap the lobstermen used to cut the smell of their work. But the odor of cinnamon and cloves, which his young mind had always associated with Aunt Sue, was gone. In its absence, the air felt stale.

"Do you want to see this or not?" Trask's gruff voice boomed from the kitchen, and Dale clenched his jaw against the memory of other shouts. Other fights.

She wouldn't have gone out at night, I know it! he'd yelled, full of grief, fury and a teenager's blind sense of justice. Trask had shouted back, *Leave me*

*alone, boy, and stop with the nonsense. They're gone.
Get used to it!*

Now, Dale walked toward the kitchen, stopping at the door and remembering how his uncle had followed the words by throwing a half-empty bottle of cheap beer. The bottle had shattered against the wall and a shard had cut deeply into his shoulder.

He'd hidden the scar with that damned tattoo and regretted the impulse for a long time after.

Trask sat at the kitchen table. Dale could picture him sitting there before, hair more yellow than white, sharing a beer with his mirror image, his younger brother, Thomas. Because the memory stung, and because Trask himself had taught Dale that emotions were weak and useless, he set his jaw and forced himself into the room. "What do you want to show us, Trask? And make it quick. We have patients to see."

He felt Tansy behind him and was grateful for her presence. There was no future for them, but she was here *now*. And it helped, though he wished it didn't.

"This," Trask said. "I wanted to show you this." He tipped out a coffee tin which had once held household pin money. Now it yielded nothing more than a few colored stones, a pretty seashell and a gold ring.

Trask's blunt fingertips plucked the ring from the table and held it up. Red and white light glinted from the facets of two gems, and Dale's throat closed. "Oh, God."

"What is it?" Tansy touched his hand and he forced himself not to reach for her. Caring was a weakness. He couldn't be weak. Not now.

Not ever.

He cleared his throat and found the words. "It's my mother's engagement ring."

"Aye." Trask, too, seemed to have trouble speaking in his normal rasp. "And from the moment my brother Thomas gave it to her, I never saw her without it. Not in the twenty years they were married. Not even once." He offered the ring to Dale. "Here, boy. It's yours."

Numbly, Dale reached for the ring, remembering how it had sat on his mother's left hand, nestled beside a matching wedding band. "Dad started saving for it on his fourteenth birthday. Even then, he knew they'd be married." The ring felt strange in his hand. Cold. Detached. He cleared his throat. "Where did you find it? On the southern claw beach?"

He winced. To think that his mother's body had washed up on shore and he hadn't known about it made Dale feel even worse.

"No." Trask shook his head. "Young Eddie found it last week." He paused. "Inland."

Dale snapped, "Impossible. She was lost at sea."

She had to have been lost at sea. If she hadn't been, then he'd failed her. He'd failed his father, and his aunt, by not staying on the island to look for them. To discover what had happened to them.

When Tansy touched his arm, Dale shook her off, pressed the heels of his hands against his temples and ground out, *"They were all lost at sea."*

"You once believed otherwise." Trask's eyes were shadowed with age and regret, but they didn't waver. "What do you believe now?"

What did he believe now? Dale almost laughed.

He believed in the power of medicine and the strength of loneliness. He believed in rights and responsibility, and in the shadowed shell of Tansy's eyelids when she used to sleep beside him.

Once, he had believed in himself. But no longer. He'd made too many mistakes, chosen wrong too many times. He'd believed Trask a hopeless drunk, but the others claimed it was a one-time thing. He'd believed he was right to chase Tansy away, knowing he didn't deserve her, knowing she wouldn't want him if she knew where he'd come from.

He'd believed…

Finally, he shook his head. "God. I don't know what to believe anymore." This time, when Tansy touched his hand he didn't shake her off. Instead, he laced his fingers between hers and hung on, drawing a measure of comfort from the contact.

She was right. He had to know what had happened to his parents.

Trask's eyes flashed. "Good. Then we're getting somewhere." He gestured to the same old chairs that still sat around the same old kitchen table. "Sit."

Tansy took the ring and held it up to the light. The

ruby glittered beside the smoky diamond, catching the wink of the stones at her wrists and ears. The ring would suit her, Dale thought, as it had suited his mother. Rich-looking. Elegant.

But the difference was, his mother had only looked rich. Tansy actually was. And he wasn't, and would never be, anything more than a lobsterman dressed in fancy linen and imported wool.

Diamonds and ugly rocks didn't mix, and Tansy was a weakness he couldn't afford, especially now. Irritated, Dale let go of her hand beneath the table, took the ring from her and handed it back to Trask.

"When did Eddie find it?" he asked, knowing the child was still in a coma. When they'd checked in at the motel a half hour earlier, Hazel said there had been no change.

Either their treatment wasn't working, or it was taking a hell of a long time. Too long, maybe. Frustration pounded at Dale's temples, and he scrubbed a hand through his hair, hoping to ease the tension but knowing it was no use.

"He found it right after the big storm that knocked out our lines to the mainland. It's been a powerful year for storms," Trask grunted. "Haven't had a storm season this bad in fifteen years."

Who the hell cared about the bloody storms? "He found it *last week?*" Dale snapped. "After all this time? That doesn't make sense. Maybe he found it in my parents' house and lied about where he was so he wouldn't get in trouble."

Trask's nostrils flared and his face darkened, as though Dale had insulted him, rather than the child. "Mickey's boy wouldn't lie about this. I'll excuse the suggestion because you're upset, but take heed. I'm warning you."

I'm warning you. Dale had heard the threat before, and its echo brought back memories of other fights, other threats. He turned away and ground the heels of his hands into his eye sockets. Pain speared through his temples, hot and vicious, reminding him how long it had been since he'd eaten. Almost a day. How long had it been since he'd slept through the night?

More than three months.

He glanced at his watch and swore when he remembered it had quit working after the plane crash. "We need to check on Eddie." He turned back to his uncle. "We'll talk later."

Though he had no idea what was left to say. Eddie couldn't possibly have found the ring inland. Not when the bodies had been lost at sea.

Trask's eyes flashed, but he nodded. "Later, then. Here," he tossed the ring in a glittering arc and Dale caught it midair. "She would have wanted you to have it."

Dale took one long look at the ring before he dropped it into his pocket, where it clinked softly against the lucky rock his mother had given him the day before she died. "Thanks, I… Thanks."

Without another word, he gestured Tansy out the

door. He needed to get away from Trask, away from the questions.

Away from the growing certainty that he'd left the island too soon, and that the oversight could mean his death—or worse, Tansy's.

DALE AND TANSY SPENT the remainder of the day at the motel clinic, monitoring the patients, drinking bottled water and flinching at shadows while the winds rose and the waves crested higher and higher against the docks. Churchill stopped in briefly to report that Hurricane Harriet was stalled off Cape Cod, so they were in for a night of gusts and not much else.

The main storm would hit the following day.

By dusk, the able-bodied islanders had finished boarding up the motel windows with sheets of plywood. Of the remaining patients, the sheriff and the mayor were failing. The young woman, Miranda, was breathing on her own, but hadn't yet regained consciousness. And Eddie was unchanged.

Then, just as the last of the gray daylight fled the sky, Dale left the motel room for a breath of stagnant, stormy air and found Mickey outside. He lifted a hand to his cousin's shoulder, not sure what to say, but knowing he needed to do something to ease the bleakness in Mickey's face.

A few minutes later, Tansy came out of the boy's room with tears in her eyes. Dale's heart stuttered.

Mickey let out a low, hopeless groan. "Is he—"

Dale reached for his cousin just as Tansy grabbed them both, turning it into an awkward three-way hug. She whispered, "He's breathing."

It took precious seconds for the words to sink in, then Mickey whooped and spun Dale nearly off his feet. "He's breathing? He's breathing! Did you hear that? He's breathing! Oh, God. Where's Libby? Where's DJ? They'll want to see Eddie!" He ran to the other end of the motel block, where his wife and older son were playing penny-ante poker.

Dale watched the quick excitement and tearful embraces, and saw Tansy smile as the entire family thundered into Unit 2, where little Eddie was finally breathing on his own.

She sighed wistfully. "They love each other so much. It's kept them strong through this."

No, Dale thought, rejecting the quick warmth he'd felt during that three-way hug, *love makes you weak. Vulnerable. Just look at what it did to Trask.*

It wasn't until he saw Tansy looking at him that he realized he'd spoken aloud.

Disappointment washed across her face, as though he'd rejected her once again. Then she stuck out her chin and snapped, "Yes, just look what love did to your uncle. Then take a good look at yourself, Dale, and tell me what you see."

The frustration in her tone punched at him, as did the sheen of tears in her eyes.

She stalked back into Eddie's room and was greeted with cheers and whoops from the excited family. But Dale didn't feel like celebrating. He wasn't sure what he felt like doing.

Feelings had never been his strong suit. Nor had communication.

Overhead, thunder grumbled. He touched the ring in his pocket and felt it clink against the stone. Both were warm from his body heat. He pulled the ring out and looked at it in the dull storm light, remembering how it had flashed on his mother's hand when she'd grabbed him around the waist and spun him in a big circle the night she died. "I've done it, Dale! I've got it! I know how we're going to send you to college!"

"Aw, Ma!" He'd shrugged her off, though there was nobody around to see her doing that touchy-feely stuff. "I don't want to go to college. I'm fine here." At seventeen, he hadn't wanted a world bigger than Lobster Island. It had been enough for every other member of his family, and it was enough for him.

"Nonsense." The ring flashed again when she took his face between her palms. As always, her hands were cool. Pie-baking hands, she'd called them— cool enough not to wreck the crusts when she kneaded them. But they were also strong enough to fight a tiller, and tough enough to dump the angry lobsters from the netted wooden traps.

She was strength wrapped in a five-foot-two package. Strength…and love.

As an adult, standing outside a falling-down motel while the muted celebration carried on without him, Dale turned his face to the darkening sky and closed his eyes. The rising storm wind was cool on his skin, like his mother's hands had been.

"Dale?"

He turned at the sound of Tansy's voice, and for a moment, her image was overlain with that of a small woman wearing a diamond and ruby ring. Then the memory was gone, and with it, his careful control disappeared.

"Dale." Tansy walked up beside him and touched his arm. "I'm sorry for what I said. I was way out of line." She took a deep breath. "And, you've said it before. It's really none of my business."

The tone of quiet defeat touched something in Dale, but he couldn't find it amidst the shame and the helpless anger towards a situation that he hadn't been able to control back then.

Seemingly couldn't control now.

"She wanted me to go to college," he said, remembering the fight, remembering his anger and her disappointment. Remembering how she'd given him his lucky stone that night and told him it was the key to his education.

Tansy stilled, and the rising breeze ruffled through her hair. "Your mother?"

He nodded. "She'd even figured out how to pay for it—though God knows how, because the storms that year were as bad as they've been this year. The catches back then were small, the money tight. Churchill didn't even own the fleet—it was just a collection of family boats barely scraping by." But he hadn't cared about the worn clothes and the third-hand jeep. It was all he'd ever known. He smiled grimly. "I wanted nothing to do with college. I was going to be a lobsterman like my father and his father. Like my uncle."

Trask. How he'd looked up to Trask, who could find the lobsters when nobody else could. He could sail faster, swim further and laugh harder than any other man on the island. How could Dale not have worshipped him?

If Trask had been on the boat that night…

Tansy touched his hand. "She got her wish, didn't she? You got your education, thanks to Churchill. I think she'd be proud."

He bared his teeth, though he knew it wasn't Tansy's fault. "Proud that I've become a rich, sanctimonious doctor, you mean? Or proud that I ran for the mainland and buried myself in school rather than sticking around long enough to find their bodies?"

Or long enough to save Trask from himself. The man was living in the past, wallowing in guilt and memories. If Dale had stayed on the island and forced his uncle to listen. . .

"I think she'd be proud that you became a doctor and joined HFH," Tansy shot back, high color staining her cheeks. "For God's sake, Dale, you were *seventeen years old*. What could you have done if you'd stayed? It's not the child's job to save the parents."

The red shame soared higher as Dale thought it bloody well *was* the duty of family to save family.

Then he saw the frantic glint in her eyes and knew she was trying to convince herself as much as him.

"This isn't about you," he snarled, emotion over-riding manners and good sense. "This isn't about poor, rich Tansy with her unfaithful father and her un-balanced mother, don't you get that? This is about *my* family, and *my* parents. We were poor, and we were happy." Shame drummed in time with his heart, but he couldn't seem to stop the shout. "Don't you get it? I failed them, not you. This isn't about you, and it isn't about us."

He felt the demons take over, heard the rage pounding in his head, or maybe that was the thunder again. He took a menacing step towards Tansy, who stood in the motel parking lot with her hands fisted at her sides, temper, grief and shocked sadness reflected in her expressive eyes. He leveled a finger at her. "I don't—"

"Stop it, Dale." Suddenly, Mickey stepped between them. "That's enough."

The brutal fist of guilt just made Dale madder. He tried to push Mickey aside, but the lobsterman held firm. Dale snapped, "Damn it, Mick, get out of my way. This isn't your business!"

"It is now." Mickey matched him glare for glare. "I'm making it my business." He glanced over his shoulder at Tansy. "She saved my boy. That makes her family, whether you like it or not. So stand down."

"Eddie's not saved yet. We won't know that until he wakes up." And in the sudden, windy silence that fell over the parking lot, Dale heard his own words. A knot jerked tight in his gut. "Oh, hell. I'm sorry, Mick."

"I'm not the one who deserves the apology," Mickey growled, glancing over toward Tansy. "She is."

But when Dale opened his mouth, she shook her head. "Don't bother. That's probably the first time you've been completely honest about your feelings. It's what I asked for all along, so there's no point in my being upset."

Her eyes were stark holes in her pale face, and her short hair moved restlessly in the rising wind. Dale felt pressure building in his chest. He wanted to shout at her and drive her away. He wanted to pull her close and never let her go. He wanted to hurt her with his words. He wanted to punish himself for hurting her.

Why did she have to be here when his world fell apart?

He took a deep breath and felt the anger, and his remaining energy, drain away. "Damn it. I didn't mean any of it. I was hurting, so I aimed where I knew I could hurt you, too. I'm sorry."

Her features didn't soften in the uncompromising lights of the dusky parking lot. "That's not the sort of thing that comes out of nowhere, Dale. There's usually at least a kernel of truth in the things we say in anger."

"What is that, one of your mother's slogans?" he snapped, then cursed and pressed the heels of his hands to his eyes. "God, I'm sorry. I need to…I need—"

"You need to turn it off for a few hours," Hazel announced, sliding an arm around Tansy's waist. "You're both exhausted. I'll stay with Eddie and the other patients. Mickey, you drop Tansy off at Churchill's mansion and take Dale home with you."

"No way." Dale scrubbed both hands across his face and could have sworn he heard the sound of his sanity cracking over the howl of the building winds. "I go where she goes. Don't forget that someone's trying to kill us."

When Hazel protested, Tansy held up a hand in the harsh light. "He's right." She glanced from Mickey to Hazel and back again. "Thanks for standing up for me, but he's right. We have to stick together for the next few days until our reinforcements arrive. No offense, but I don't know who to trust on this island." Her eyes slid to Dale. "Dale and I have our problems, but he doesn't want me dead."

The subtext read, *Dale doesn't want me at all.* He winced, but didn't bother to contradict her. It was what he wanted her to think, after all.

Wasn't it?

THEY BORROWED MICKEY'S jeep and rode to Churchill's place in silence, not even commenting when they passed the burned, wrecked house that had once belonged to Dale's parents. The vehicle bounced and slid along the dirt road, and Tansy gritted her teeth to keep from cursing when each bump sang up her spine.

She ached from head to toe. Her back hurt from the hours she'd spent bending over the motel beds, administering the sticky coconut and brown sugar mixture to the patients. Her feet hurt where the borrowed shoes pinched, and her eyes stung with the memory of smoke and fire from the night before. That was why they burned, she told herself, not because of what Dale had said.

She *wasn't* a poor little rich girl. And even if she was, then what did that make Dale?

A poor match, whispered a voice in the back of her head, and Tansy closed her eyes. She hadn't wanted to believe it, not after everything they'd meant to each other. Not after everything he'd meant to her.

He parked the jeep in Churchill's carefully raked clamshell drive and sat for a moment, hands gripping the steering wheel, eyes staring straight out into the night, which had fallen with a heavy, stormy abruptness. Lacking the energy for another fight, Tansy reached for the door handle.

His voice came out of the darkness, carrying across the intimate little space like a caress. "Tans…I really am sorry for what I said." He was silhouetted against the lit front of the mansion, and light glinted off his hair when he turned toward her. "You hit a nerve. I'd been sitting there, thinking of all the things I did wrong, all the things I could've done differently…and there you were, like my conscience."

Tansy's own conscience nagged at her with the knowledge that she'd slapped at him while he was reeling from Trask's revelations. That hadn't been fair, or wise, but there had never been a middle ground for them. It was always either excitement or anger, love or hate. Nothing in between.

She opened the door and jumped from the jeep, clenching her teeth when the jolt sang through her tired body. "It's okay, Dale. Let's just forget about it."

He followed her to the front door and held it open. The light from the entryway spilled out onto them, gilding his white-blond hair and clear blue eyes. Tansy's chest ached with the realization that if they survived the storm, they'd never have to see each other again. They'd be going in different directions, still wanting different things.

She wanted a family. He wanted anything but. She wanted honesty. To him, that meant only pain.

A bad match.

"It's not okay," he replied. He closed the door behind them, shutting out the night and the storm. Shutting out the stranger who had set a trip wire across their landing strip and burned Dale's house to the ground. "But I'm going to make it okay. I'm going to get you out of here safely, Tansy, I swear it on my mother's grave."

His mother's empty grave.

Tansy shook off the thought and headed for the stairs. "I'm not your responsibility, Dale." She'd wanted to be so much more, and he'd only been able to offer less. Her eyes stung with smoke and tears. "I'm going to take a bath."

When you need to cry, her mother had always told her, *find someplace private. Men don't like tears.*

Well, Tansy didn't give a flip what Dale thought about tears, but she needed the time alone.

Upstairs, while filling Churchill's luxurious guest bath, she tried to relax, and failed. She tried to let the tears come, but they wouldn't. Her mind kept returning to the exquisite pain on Dale's face when he'd watched Mickey with his wife and children. There had been a moment of longing, she was sure of it. Then he'd shut it off and scowled.

"Oh, Dale," she whispered over the sound of water pouring into the tub and the wail of the wind outside. She shivered inside her fluffy robe.

"Tans? You okay in there?" His muffled words came through the wooden panel, as though he, too, recognized the new distance between them and was afraid to even crack the door.

She walked to the carved wood and imagined him leaning against the other side. She pressed her hand to the place his face might be. "I'm fine," she said softly. "Just fine."

But it was a lie. She wasn't fine. She hurt for him. Hurt for herself.

"Can I get you anything?" He must have realized she was beside the door, because his voice came through low and intimate.

Three months ago, or even three hours ago, she might have damned the consequences and invited him to share her bath. But not now. She shook her head, though he couldn't see the motion. "No, thanks. I'm fine."

But, oh, the temptation ached through her body. She knew the places he could take her, the things he could make her forget. Worse, she knew the sensations he would force her to remember. And now?

Now she'd have to forget them for a lifetime.

She heard Dale's sigh through the layer of wood. Finally, he said, "I'll be out here, keeping watch."

When he moved away from the door, Tansy stayed there a moment with her hand pressed to the cool wood, feeling the steam close around her and hearing the tone of the rushing water change as the tub filled. But still, she couldn't cry. Instead, determination built within her, chasing away the weakness and the self-pity. She could help Dale. Damn it, she *would* help Dale, whether he wanted her assistance or not.

A car door slammed and a dog barked. Hearing Churchill and Frankie's voices outside her open window, Tansy bathed quickly and pulled her borrowed clothes back on.

In the bedroom, she found Dale sprawled across the bed, fully dressed. He was fast asleep. She paused, caught by the frown that hadn't smoothed from his face, even in sleep.

His shirt was half open, and in the light spilling from the bathroom, the shadow of the lobster tattoo was a dark patch against his smooth skin. She couldn't stop herself from crossing the big room and touching the place where the faded ink covered his heart. Though she had no right, she leaned down and kissed him softly on the lips, feeling a sharp sliver of pain when he smiled in his sleep.

She longed to climb into that big bed, snuggle up beside him and pretend none of this was happening. Instead, she turned away and tiptoed from the room.

Downstairs, Churchill was alone in the kitchen. When Tansy marched into the room, he paused in the act of assembling a sandwich. His eyes lit with approval. "Good evening, Dr. Whitmore. I hear your cure has brought some miracles."

It took her a moment to remember that Eddie was breathing on his own. The event, which should have been a triumph, had been lost amid the rest of the day. She smiled at the memory of Mickey and his family hanging over the motel bed, watching Eddie's color return. "Hopefully, he'll regain consciousness tomorrow."

Churchill smiled. "That's wonderful!" He gestured to the counter, where he'd spread the makings of a late dinner. "You must be hungry. What can I offer you?"

Tansy took a deep breath and sat. "I'll have whatever you're having. Then I want you to tell me about Dale's parents and the *Curly Sue*."

Chapter Eight

Churchill frowned, pulled a second plate down from a high cupboard and set about making her a sandwich. "There's not much to tell. Lobstering is a tough business, and the North Atlantic waters are treacherous this far offshore. It's a rare year when we don't lose at least one boat and her crew."

He set the sandwich in front of her and took his seat, sliding a plate of cookies between them. Tansy dug into her sandwich as he continued, "Kristin, Thomas and Suzie were fine people, and good friends. I mourned them." Churchill took a cookie and nibbled at one corner. "But as for Trask's talk of murder?" He shook his head. "Even if Eddie found Kristin's engagement ring inland, I don't see how that 'proves' anything. Besides, they were good people. Who would want them dead?"

"That's what I'm trying to figure out," Tansy replied between bites. "But someone wants to get Dale off the island, either by scaring him away or by—" she swallowed hard "—killing him." Us. "That seems like pretty good evidence that foul play was covered up, and that the perpetrator doesn't want Dale nosing around."

"Or…" Churchill looked worried, and from his position beneath the table, the Doberman whined. "Hush, Janus. It's okay." He passed a piece of cookie to the dog and continued. "Or else the plane crash and the fire weren't specifically aimed at Dale."

"Yes," Tansy admitted, "I'd thought of that, too." A big shudder crawled down her back. Churchill covered her hand with his own and she didn't move away, needing that moment of contact. Though the older man was a stranger, Dale trusted him. Right now, that would have to be enough for her. "But who would want to hurt us? Someone with a grudge against HFH? That seems unlikely, which means that it has to be someone who wants…"

Outside, a harder gust of wind hit the mansion, rattling the storm shutters and the front door. Tansy flinched, and Churchill finished her thought. "Someone who wants the outbreak to continue. Someone who has a vested interest in islanders moving to the mainland."

Roberts. He didn't say it, but the real estate developer's name hung between them like a curse.

The front door banged again, and this time, over the howl of the rising wind, they heard a man shouting. "Churchill? Frankie?"

It was Mickey's voice.

Oh, God. Not again. Half-panicked, Tansy shot to

her feet and ran for the door with Churchill and the Doberman at her heels. She flung the door open and raised her voice over the howls of the wind. "Mickey! Is it Eddie?"

She hoped for the best. She feared the worst. But Dale's cousin, wild-eyed and rumpled from sleeping in his clothes three days running, shook his head. "No, not Eddie!" A strong gust nearly toppled the big man, and he reached for her. "It's Hazel."

Panic iced to horror, closing Tansy's throat. *Hazel!*

"What happened to her?" asked Dale's voice from behind her. She turned to find him halfway down the curving staircase, wearing jeans and nothing else. The faded lobster tattoo crossed his heart, standing out in dark relief against his skin. The worn denim sagged across his hipbones, seeming held up more by habit than by a waistband. Lean, sinewy muscles crowded one atop the other in sculpted layers of hard male flesh.

His eyes flickered to her, then away, and he repeated his question. "Mickey. What happened to Hazel?"

There was a brief lull in the wind, and in the sudden, eerie quiet, the lobsterman's words seemed overly loud.

"She was attacked."

TANSY CLUTCHED THE ROLL bar as Dale sent the jeep skidding into the motel parking lot. He stalled the engine and they raced across the parking lot, eyes slitted against blowing sand.

Raised voices carried from the half-open door to Unit 2. "Damn it! I want you to go home, woman! Why are you being so bloody stubborn?"

Dale cursed and punched the door fully open. "Leave her alone, Trask. Can't you do anything without shouting at people?"

The almost-combatants froze. Hazel was seated beside Eddie's bed, holding an ice pack to the side of her face. Trask loomed over her, breathing hard. Tansy wondered whether Dale could see the fear in the older man's eyes, whether he understood it. Probably not, she thought with a shimmer of disappointment. No doubt he saw the anger and missed the love.

Trask surged to his feet, a dull red flush climbing the back of his neck. "This is none of your business, boy."

Dale took a menacing step forward, and Tansy decided she'd had enough. Enough of this island, enough of Alice down the rabbit hole, and more than enough of Dale and his uncle. Like a pair of bulls, they were too busy pawing and snorting at each other to realize their energy would be better spent elsewhere. Like investigating Roberts, who would profit if the island's economy collapsed.

"Out!" she snapped, pointing to the door. "This is a hospital room. If you need to fight, do it outside, so I can tend Hazel and check on Eddie. If you're going to stay, then behave, both of you!"

Surprisingly, shouting worked.

Dale raised his eyebrows and stepped back, leaving Tansy wondering whether she should have started yelling a long time ago. Even during their worst fights, she'd always treated him as an equal, as an adult capable of making rational decisions. Maybe that had been her mistake.

New, unfamiliar power surged through her. *Keep your man happy and he won't stray,* her mother had said, so Tansy had tried. She'd tried to keep him stocked with clean underwear in the field and expensive wines at home, but it hadn't been good enough. *She* hadn't been good enough.

Now, she wondered whether she hadn't been tough enough.

Trask glowered, and shuffled his feet. "The woman takes a punch in the face and won't go home to lie down. What am I supposed to do?"

Giving her some sympathy would be a nice place to start, Tansy thought as she knelt beside Hazel's chair. *Maybe some cuddling and a shoulder to cry on.* But that would never happen. Trask and Dale were too alike that way. Too unemotional. Too closed off. How could a woman ever really know a man like that?

She couldn't, that was the answer.

Irritated with her thoughts, and with the men, she shook her head and focused on her newest patient. "What happened?"

The older doctor pulled the ice pack away from her swollen, red cheek. A tendril of soft gray hair curled across her jaw, making her look younger, vulnerable. "I stepped outside for a breath of air." Finding solace in the familiar actions, Tansy performed a routine check and found no injuries beyond the blow to Hazel's face, as the other woman continued, "It was twilight, and he was dressed in black."

"He?" Dale asked quickly. "Did you see his face?"

"No. It was dark, and the wind had knocked over one of the lights in the parking lot, so I left them all off." She gestured outside the open door, where the bare bulbs, were now lit. "Obviously, we turned them on after the attack."

Tansy thought the feeble light and the flickering, neon No Vacancy sign made the area look creepier than no light at all. The shadows were elongated and strangely colored. Perfect for hiding. The windows were all boarded against the storm.

Perfect for an attacker to do his business, with no-body to hear the screams over the winds of the coming hurricane.

She shivered at the thought of what might have happened to Hazel. What might already have happened to her and Dale.

Hazel continued, "I had just decided to check on Miranda when I heard a noise behind me. I turned, and *wham!*" She slapped her palms together, and both Dale and Trask winced. "He knocked me down. I fell against the biohazard garbage cans outside, and I think the noise scared him away. He took off around the back of the motel just as Trask pulled up." Hazel cut her eyes to the older man. "Trask chased the man, but there was too much of a head start."

"Did he say anything?" Dale snapped, clearly frustrated with the vague description. When she shook her head, he cursed. "What the hell did he want?"

"What do you think he wants, Dale?" Tansy demanded, her temper spiking. "He wants you or me dead. Or maybe he was willing to include Hazel on his list. Are you the target? Is this about your parents? If so, why hasn't he gone after Trask? Or is this about the outbreak? How much do we really know about this developer fellow? He's the only outsider on the island."

"I—" Dale started to answer automatically, then paused, considering. "You know, those are good questions."

Questions they hadn't asked or answered before because they had been so busy arguing emotions.

Suddenly it was overwhelming. The plane crash and the house fire, the outbreak and the attack on Hazel. Tansy didn't understand what was happening, and what little she knew about the island, or her partner's place on it, had come from carefully hoarded details or information from the others. Dale had told her nothing. And because of the things he hadn't told her, someone wanted her dead. *She didn't understand.* Her temper bubbled higher. "How can you expect me to do my job if *you won't tell me what's going on?*"

Dale held out a hand. "Tansy, calm down. We need to—"

"Tell me!" she interrupted. "Tell me about your island, and about the people on it." She was getting louder and she didn't care. "Or would that violate the 'nobody gets close to Dale Metcalf' rule? You bring me here, you put me in danger, and now you won't tell me what's going on. Damn you, I deserve better!"

When she stopped, breathing hard, Tansy realized all three of them were staring at her in silence. Even the wind had died down, leaving the plywood-shrouded room echoing with quiet. A fierce red heat burned its way up her throat as she heard her own words vibrate on the still air.

God, she sounded just like her mother.

Who were you with this time, Richard? Where were you? How can you do this to me over and over again? Tell me...I deserve better!

Only, her mother had always shouted those questions at her daughter, or into an empty room. She'd never asked her husband. She'd never dared.

Well, Tansy dared, all right. She narrowed her eyes at Dale. "And don't even *think* about walking away or changing the subject this time, Metcalf. Don't try it."

He stared back at her, and for the first time since before they'd become lovers, Tansy felt as though he was actually *looking* at her. Actually seeing her. She felt a quick moment of hope, then he turned away and muttered. "I didn't want you here in the first place."

Her heart sank and her brief, righteous anger spluttered and died. They were back to this, then. "Okay. Fine." She jutted her chin out. "I'm out of here on the first plane that lands after the storm."

It was a lie. She would never leave her partner in danger. She'd stay on Lobster Island as long as he did. She'd watch his back and trust him to watch hers. But in her heart, she finally gave up on him. On them. She might love a man who didn't love her enough. But damn it, she would keep her pride.

Dale stared at her for a tense moment, his eyes, as always, unreadable. Finally, he cursed and turned to Trask. "Take Hazel home with you," he commanded, "Tansy and I will stay with the patients."

"She won't come with me," Trask grumbled, and Tansy saw a flash of hurt in his eyes. "She hates my house."

Dale blew out an exasperated breath. "Hazel? I don't want you staying alone, until the storm passes and help arrives." He jerked his chin toward the room next door. "With the sheriff and the mayor both on respirators, we don't have any official, legal backup, understand? We have to look out for each other, which means you're going home with Trask."

Hazel shot the older man an irritated look that was foiled somewhat by the bruise spreading out from beneath the ice pack. "I don't hate your house, Trask. I hate the furnishings. I hate that you haven't changed a thing in fifteen years. It's like you're still waiting for her to walk through the door and pick up where she left off."

Trask stalked to the open door and glared out into the eerily lit parking lot. "I'm not waiting for Suzie to come home." He cracked his work-gnarled knuckles. "I know she's gone. But I'm a poor man. I don't have the money for foolish things like redecorating."

"I know you, Trask," Hazel replied quietly. "If you wanted to change things, you'd find a way."

When he didn't respond, her eyes welled with quickly hidden tears. Tansy felt an answering tug in her chest and suddenly needed to escape Dale's presence. She needed time alone to think. She cleared her throat. "I'll take Hazel to her place. Dale can monitor the patients."

He shook his head in quick, definitive denial. "No. I'm not letting you out of my sight." He turned to his uncle. "Trask, you take Hazel to her house. Tansy and I will stay with the patients."

"But, Dale—"

"No buts, Tansy. I mean it." His blue eyes were hard, implacable. She flinched under their impact. "You wouldn't be here if it weren't for me. That makes you my responsibility."

"That's bull and you know it," she answered automatically as her stubborn, foolish heart clenched in her chest. She didn't want to be his responsibility. She wasn't sure *what* she wanted from him anymore.

"Bull or not, that's the way it is." He gestured Trask and a reluctant Hazel out the door. When they were gone, the room was silent, save for the sigh of the wind outside. Dale stood in the doorway, the yellow light of Eddie's makeshift hospital room lighting one side of him, the flickering, parking lot neon lighting the other. The anger in the room dissipated quickly, leaving another energy behind.

After a long moment, Tansy turned away. "Why don't you check on the other patients? I want to set up another run on the chromatograph." They still hadn't confirmed the nature of the toxicity. Too many other things had interfered. She tried for a smile. "If we make it out of here, this outbreak should be written up for the journals, at any rate."

"You're right," he answered quietly. He crossed the room to stand behind her, a breath away, and she knew he wasn't talking about the experiment now. "You're right about all of it. I should have told you about this place a long time ago. I should have told you about my parents, and about Trask and Churchill."

Tansy concentrated on donning a pair of surgical gloves and preparing a sample of Eddie's blood for testing. Part of her leaped gladly that he was *talking* to her, finally talking to her. But the smarter part of her said it was too little, too late. "Why didn't you?"

He blew out a breath, but he didn't move away. "I don't know. It was just…easier to tell myself that you wouldn't understand Lobster Island."

"Because my parents had money."

He turned her to face him, and the familiar warmth radiated from the place where his fingers touched her skin. "Be realistic, Tansy. You deserve marble bathtubs and silk sheets, not this place." His gesture encompassed the paper-thin walls and the surplus carpeting.

She didn't bother to point out that he was fifteen years and two university degrees removed from the poverty, nor did she remind him that they'd spent most of their time together on assignments in sorrier places than the motel. She simply linked her hands around his wrists, where they rested on her shoulders. "We'll never know, will we? You never gave it a chance." Seeing cool wariness creep into his eyes, she sighed. "No, don't worry. I'm not asking you for more. I'm finally accepting that you can't give it to me."

"Meaning?" His eyes were chilly, but behind the mask, she thought she might have seen a hint of panic.

No, that was her imagination, Tansy decided over the knell of her heart. This is what he wanted. She stuck out her chin. "Meaning I'm done. You've made it clear you want nothing to do with the sorts of emotions that Trask has gone through. Fine. You've got your wish. As soon as HFH can get a plane here, I'm gone. I'll tell them to find you a new partner—preferably a man."

His eyes darkened. "Tansy, I never meant to—"

"I know," she interrupted quickly before her resolve could give. "It's okay." And to show just how okay it was, she leaned up on tiptoes and pressed her lips to his, intending to show him that it was truly over between them.

The action was a terrible, terrible mistake.

Her mind was trying to say "goodbye," but her body gave a great, joyous cry of welcome when their lips touched. Dale started in surprise, and the sweep of heat warned Tansy that she had wandered back into her mother's world of chemistry over common sense. She started to pull away, but was too late. Dale's fingers dug into her shoulders once before he slid his hands down to gather her close.

In an instant, her goodbye became the sort of hello that had blinded her to reason so many times before. When his quiet, desperate groan shivered through her, she opened her mouth to him, and tried to keep her heart locked tight.

His taste brought memories that were instantly swept away by the newness of it. The coarse wool beneath her fingertips was unfamiliar, as was the faint rasp of stubble across her cheek. Unfamiliar, and wildly erotic.

She murmured something needy. Her head shouted for her to push him away, though her arms urged him closer. His tongue swept inside her mouth and desire swirled, fierce and fiery, only fanned higher by the gusting wind outside and the grumble of thunder overhead.

Or perhaps that was her heart.

In the field, Dale had been an inventive, uninhibited lover. At home, less so. But the man she kissed now was neither of those people. He tasted of primal, uncivilized urges. She murmured agreement when his fingers dug tighter into her shoulders.

And a small voice behind her said, "Ma? Pa? DJ?"

IT TOOK PRECIOUS SECONDS for Dale's eyes to focus on the boy in the motel bed and comprehend that—

wonder of wonders—Eddie was awake. It took longer for him to force himself to let go of Tansy.

Ever since he'd realized, in the middle of an earthquake relief effort four months earlier, that he'd go mad if anything ever happened to her, he'd tried to hold her at arm's length. Then she'd kissed him, and all rational thought had fled, and with it, all of his reasons for keeping her away. His heart still beat a heavy tattoo, and his chest still swirled with a poignant combination of greed and regret. It wasn't just lust. No, that would be too easy.

It was Tansy. And that was the most complicated thing in the world.

"Ma?" At the sight of two near-strangers, little Eddie's face crumpled. "Pa?" He darted blue-eyed glances at the shabby motel room, with its plywood covered windows, and cringed away from the respirator, which sill rested near his bed. Finally, he locked wide, frightened eyes on Tansy and whispered, "You're the ghost lady. Am I dead?"

"No, Eddie, you're not dead." Tansy dropped her arms from around Dale's neck. Dull red climbed her cheeks. "You're fine." She perched on the edge of the boy's bed and brushed a strand of blond hair off his forehead.

"Where's my ma and pa?" the boy demanded, his voice growing rapidly stronger. "Where's DJ?" Worry clouded his face. "They're okay, right?"

"They're fine," Tansy assured him. "They'll be here in a minute."

Her gesture sent Dale for the door. He was glad to escape the room, and the pressure on his chest. He had always been strangely unsettled to see how good Tansy was with children and to think that she must want her own. Once, he'd told himself it worried him because he didn't like kids much. But in all honesty, he loved the little monsters. He just didn't want his own. It had been hard enough to lose his parents.

He didn't want to imagine losing a child. Or a wife.

He took one last look back at Tansy, who was bent over Eddie, listening to him while checking his vitals. Then he turned and walked out into the rising storm, and shut the door behind him.

A voice spoke from the shadows near the jeep. "Dr. Metcalf? Is everything okay?"

Dale jolted and spun, remembering Hazel's attack and knowing that Tansy was alone in the motel room with a sick little boy. "Who is it?"

A figure stepped into the washy neon light and held out a hand. "We haven't been properly introduced. I'm Nat Roberts." He was wearing a white shirt atop navy trousers and black shoes. A dark blue zip-up jacket was slung over his shoulder.

He was dressed in black, Hazel had said. Or perhaps navy?

Dale ignored the hand. "No, everything's not okay. Dr. Hazel was attacked about an hour ago. You wouldn't know anything about that, would you?"

Roberts scowled. "Not you, too? And here I thought since you'd spent some time on the mainland, you'd be above the islanders' conviction that I'm the boogeyman." He snorted. "It's not my fault the lobstering's gone bad. I'm their ticket off this miserable rock, not that any of them will thank me for it."

Dale wondered at Roberts's lack of surprise. Then again, given the island grapevine, it was just as likely he'd heard of Hazel's attack secondhand, even this late at night. Still, the developer had said it himself—anything that was bad for the lobstering business was good for him. The storms. The disease. All of it.

Apparently taking the silence for suspicion, Roberts sighed. "I have an alibi. I was visiting a few of the more stubborn holdouts." He patted his back pocket. "I have signed agreements from two of them. Three others slammed their doors in my face, but they'll come around. Face it, this island's dying."

A week earlier, Dale might have cheered to learn that Lobster Island had sunk into the ocean. Now, he narrowed his eyes. "Nobody and nothing is dying on my watch." Except maybe the mayor, who was reportedly one of Roberts's biggest foes at the town meetings that had been called to discuss the buyout. "Who signed tonight?" When Roberts hesitated, Dale ground out, "This is your alibi, buddy, not mine."

The developer muttered an unkind word and offered the signed papers. Dale flipped through them and froze at the second signature.

Walter Churchill.

"This is a fake," he snapped, unable to believe that Walter would sell out.

Roberts didn't even bristle. He grinned. "It's real. It seems the tycoon of Lobster Island is having more financial troubles than he's letting on. Besides, I think he's ready to escape this smelly excuse for an island and get back to the real world. Our offer was more than generous, and it locks up the forty percent of the island he controls."

Forty percent. Damn. Churchill must've bought out every islander that had left in the past decade. He'd finally burned out his resources. Dale fought the urge to crumple the contract, instead returning it to Roberts. "Fine. But don't go anywhere. I'm going to have a few more questions for you later."

Roberts shrugged. "Where would I go? Haven't you heard? There's a hurricane coming. Until it's past, we're all trapped here." And he was gone, slipping eel-like through the door to Unit 1, the only one the islanders hadn't boarded up.

After a brief, intense internal debate, Dale knocked on the door to the small cottage beside the motel. Once a sleepy lobster sorter agreed to fetch Eddie's parents, Dale returned to the motel.

There was no way in hell he was leaving Tansy alone there with Roberts around.

BY THE TIME DALE RETURNED, Tansy had herself back under control. It did her no good to make grand, sweeping statements about her independence, then practically crawl inside his skin when she tried to kiss him goodbye.

She frowned, then consciously smoothed her expression as she sat down beside Eddie once more. "How are you feeling, sweetie?"

"Okay, Miss Tansy," Eddie replied with a sleepy half smile. They had established an uneasy bond once she'd assured him that she wasn't a ghost, and that he was in the motel, not heaven. The kid had an imagination, she'd give him that.

"How's he doing?" Dale asked. Since returning from the parking lot, he'd been prowling the little room, adjusting dials that didn't need adjusting.

"He seems okay. Are the others coming?" She slid over when Dale crouched beside the bed and his leg brushed against hers.

"They're on their way." He turned to the boy. "Hey, Eddie. Before your family gets here, can you tell us where you were before you got sick? It's pretty important."

So far, Eddie was the only patient to regain consciousness. Maybe he could provide them a badly needed clue as to the source of the toxicity. Tansy held her breath.

Eddie scrunched his face up, concentrating, but it was clear that his strength was already fading. "I was at the ghost house with DJ."

She patted his hand. "Yes, we saw you there. But your tummy was already hurting, remember? Where were you before you started feeling sick?"

"I was looking for the river." His eyelids eased shut. "The river where I found the pretty ring." Like turning out a light, he was asleep in a breath. His body needed the rest after its prolonged fight.

Tansy checked his pulse while she processed the new information. She didn't like the conclusion she came up with. "He found the ring in or near a river, right after one of the big storms." She glanced at Dale to see if his mind had wandered in a similar direction as hers. The tense set of his jaw suggested that it had.

"They said they were going for a walk that night," he ground out. He stood and walked to the doorway, stared out into the night.

A quick chill skittered through Tansy. "Your parents and your aunt?"

He nodded. Pain etched sharp lines across his forehead and beside his mouth. "There was no reason for them to go out on the boat. My mother hated being out on the water after dark. But there was something she wanted to show my father—something she and Suzie had found that day." He swallowed. "Inland. Near a river."

"Maybe she dropped the ring while they were walking," Tansy said, feeling goose bumps march up her arms and wishing she could spare him from the other conclusion, the obvious conclusion. "Maybe the rains washed it down from where it fell."

His lips flattened to a thin line. "Or else it washed down from something else."

A grave.

Chapter Nine

The mayor died at midnight, the sheriff not long after.

Tansy felt the failure like an open wound. They should have done more. Been faster. Figured it out sooner. Ever since they'd arrived on the island, she'd felt two steps behind the pace. Two steps behind the outbreak. Two steps behind the faceless shadow that wanted them dead.

Sitting beside her on the cracked sidewalk outside Eddie's room, Dale muttered a curse.

Like the wind and the grumble of thunder that had moved far offshore, Tansy had felt frustration building in him through the night. He was so angry, so unhappy, so worried for her and for the people he was—maybe—coming to see as his family. Wishing she knew how to help him, wishing she didn't feel the need to help him, Tansy touched his clenched fist and was surprised when he grabbed her hand and held on tight.

Warmth invaded her chest at the thought that he needed something from her, but she quickly banished the soft emotion. He'd made it plain that he neither wanted nor needed what they once had together.

A faint beeping from Eddie's room brought her to her feet before she recognized the tone. It wasn't one of the boy's monitors—he was sleeping peacefully now, not hooked to a single machine. No, this beep came from the chromatograph. It had finished running the sample of Eddie's blood.

Dale rose. "Now we'll know for sure." But neither of them moved.

If the chromatogram showed a series of jagged peaks, there was a good chance the poisoning came from a natural source. Each outbreak of PSP showed a different blend of toxins, with a few core molecules that caused the main effects. But if, as they had come to suspect without really saying it, the outbreak was man-made, it seemed likely that the killer would use purified saxitoxin—the most deadly of those core molecules.

One peak or many? Suddenly, Tansy was reluctant to find out for sure. While the experiment would answer one question, it would pose so many new ones, including the most important one of all: who had poisoned the islanders, and why?

It had to be someone on the island. Roberts was the obvious suspect. He was an outsider, and they could even stretch to give him motive. But Tansy wasn't sure.

It didn't quite feel right.

"You ready?" Coming to her out of the darkness,

Dale's voice slid along her nerve endings and caressed her storm-cooled skin.

She nodded, and they walked into the motel room together, interrupting the quiet vigil of Trask, Hazel and Mickey, who sat around the boy's bedside, watching him breathe. Waiting for him to wake up again.

Trask and Dale traded glares. Little had been settled between the two, and they had lapsed into a wary standoff that Tansy found just as exhausting as their earlier battles. Then again, she thought, little good came of families, feuding or otherwise. Just look at her parents, and—

And she was stalling. Beside her, Dale hadn't moved either. It was as though neither of them wanted the final confirmation of what they all knew.

She blamed exhaustion for the fine tremble of her fingers when she ripped the printout from the chromatograph. There was silence in the room as she scanned it. Even the wind and the thunder had gone quiet.

Finally, Dale asked, "One or many?"

The single large peak looked like a mountain, or maybe an accusatory finger. A grave marker. Tansy shuddered and handed the paper to Dale. "One."

He cursed. "Then it's murder."

Murder. It shouldn't have been shocking, but the word cut through the little room with scalpel sharpness.

"But who?" asked Hazel, reaching for Trask's hand.

"My bet is on Roberts," Tansy replied.

After a moment, Trask nodded. "The people he

works for want the island, one way or the other, is that it?"

"Perhaps," Dale agreed, staring down at the paper. "But it still feels as though we're missing something."

Tansy wasn't surprised he felt it, too. She touched his arm. "Do you think it has anything to do with your parents?"

He shifted away. "No." He shot a glance at his uncle, as though daring him to contradict. "That was then, this is now. The attempts on Tansy's and my life—and Hazel's attack—have been to keep us from solving the outbreak, nothing more. Nobody cares about—" his voice caught on the words "—about three people who died fifteen years ago. That's ancient history. We need to focus on what's happening here and now."

The fading breeze sighed through the open door, a sad, lonely sound that gathered beneath Tansy's breastbone like a weight.

"This *is* the here and now, boy." Trask stood and squared off against Dale. "Your parents are the here and now, and my Suzie. What's happening now is because of what happened back then, I'd swear to it."

"You'd swear to a lot of things," Hazel snapped, rising from her chair and facing the older man, "not the least of which is that Suzie was the best part of you. Well, I know better than that, Trask, but I'm also figuring out that you know it, too. It's just easier for you to dwell on the past than it is to figure out the future. Well, to hell with that. And to hell with you."

She stalked out of the room and into the night, which was still and silent. Waiting.

Trask followed her to the door and bellowed, "Hazel? Hazel, get back in here!" When she just kept marching and passed beneath the flickering neon, he cursed. "I'm going after her." Halfway out the door, he turned back. "Keep your woman and the boy safe, Dale. We'll meet again in the morning to make a plan. If Roberts is behind this, we need to stop him before anyone else is hurt."

It wasn't exactly an apology, but it was close. Dale must have thought the same thing, because he murmured, "That's the first time he's called me by name since that night."

Tansy touched his arm, and this time he didn't move away. "He's right, we should rest." She didn't want to talk about Dale's uncle, or about the flash of vulnerability she'd seen on both their faces. She didn't want to talk about the danger, or the deaths they hadn't been able to prevent.

Most of all, Tansy didn't want to talk about Hazel's outburst, or the sad, unflinching parallels between them, two women irrevocably drawn to men who couldn't be bothered to love them.

"And he's also right that we need to stay safe tonight." Dale nudged the door shut with his toe and shot the bolt, locking the two adults and the sleeping boy into the small, intimate room. "Why don't you get some sleep and I'll take the first watch."

"Okay. I'll just…" Feeling the small room close

in on her, Tansy gestured to the bathroom and es-
caped, feeling a hot blush burn her cheeks. She
shouldn't be so foolish. She'd sworn off Dale, hadn't
she? So why was it suddenly almost unbearable for
her to be trapped in a shabby hotel room with him
for the night?

Because, she realized, this was likely one of the
last nights they'd ever spend together. And because
of the barriers she'd seen stripped from his soul, one
by one, over the past few days. At Boston General,
Dale was the social loner, always surrounded by
friends he never let close. Here, he had discovered
his family, and didn't seem sure whether he wanted
them or not.

It was stupid for her to hope that he'd learn to love
his family. That he'd learn to love her.

But Whitmore women, as well as being foolish in
love, were also incurable optimists. The pathologies
went hand in hand.

"Well, not this time," Tansy muttered. She ignored
the beckoning shower and splashed cold water on her
face, hoping to dampen the heat that had climbed the
moment Dale locked them in together. "You can do
this," she told herself, "you can be strong."

Out in the main room, she found him crouched
over the pile of battered, salt-encrusted cases they'd
pulled from the harbor. Willing her voice steady, she
said, "Most everything beyond the chromatograph
was a write-off, and I'm not even sure we'd get another reading out of it."

"Yeah, but this might work." Dale leaned to one side, and she saw the contents of the open case. A huge shiver crawled down her neck at the sight of the shotgun every HFH team was required to carry. Most teams left the weapon on the plane rather than taking it along, knowing that in the places HFH visited, guns often brought more harm than good.

Every now and then, though, HFH doctors had been forced to defend their work or their persons. Hurting to heal.

Dale racked a shell into the chamber, and Tansy shuddered. But she didn't ask whether the precaution was necessary.

"Do you think it'll fire?" she asked, perching on the spare bed, the one Eddie wasn't using, and feeling the mattress give beneath her. The softness reminded her just how tired she was, just how little sleep they'd gotten in the past few days.

"It looks like it stayed dry," he replied, but he didn't sound certain. "I guess we can test fire it out over the water in the morning." He stood and faced her, his eyes unreadable. "Until then..."

She nodded. "Until then, we'll keep it close and hope we don't need it."

There was a long pause, and their eyes locked. Heat flared between them. Dale swallowed hard and reached out a hand to touch her cheek. His finger traced along the curve of her jaw, and Tansy felt something rise into her throat. She wasn't sure if it was a scream or a sob or a prayer—she just knew she couldn't handle this, couldn't handle him, and that she was in danger of losing hold of her resolve.

Then he quickly backed away, fetching up against the door frame. "Get some sleep."

The order was sharp, the husky quality of his voice anything but. Helpless against the feelings, the memories and the knowledge it would soon be over, Tansy held out a hand. "Dale—"

He flicked the wall switch, plunging the room into complete darkness broken only by the faint neon light that oozed through the cracks between the plywood sheets. After a moment, Tansy's eyes adjusted, and she could pick out the angle of Dale's cheek, the plane of his jaw. As though he could feel her watching him, he turned and stared toward the bed. "Go to sleep, Tans. I'll keep watch."

After a moment, he returned his attention to the sliver of the parking lot visible through the crack.

"Do you see anything?" she asked quietly, grateful for the darkness and the opportunity to stare at him unobserved. She felt, more than saw, the gun at his side. It seemed to radiate mechanical malevolence and safety at the same time, and it surprised Tansy to find its presence eased her.

He shook his head, and his hair was illuminated in shades of red, then blue and yellow as it caught different shafts of reflected neon. "No, nothing." Roberts had gone to his room just after dark, and none of them had seen or heard from the man since. It was a relief to know where he was, but it gave Tansy the sense of an evil, waiting presence just on the other side of the motel's paper-thin wall. She shivered slightly and lay down on her side, still watching Dale.

He would keep her safe, she knew, or die trying. That was the sort of man he was.

Too bad he didn't trust the fact.

After a long moment, he spoke again. "Looks like the wind is dying down. Maybe the storm is going to miss us."

"Maybe," she answered.

But she knew neither of them believed it.

FINALLY, AFTER WHAT FELT like days, but was only forty minutes by the faint glow of Dale's watch, Tansy fell asleep. He could sense it in the subtle softening of the tension that hung in the room, and he heard it in that last sweet gasp she always gave right before succumbing to oblivion. His Tansy, stubborn to the end, fought sleep as if it was her enemy, only falling when there was no other option.

Except she wasn't "his Tansy" anymore. He'd seen it in her eyes, the final understanding they weren't meant to be together, the final acceptance that they were too different, too unsuited for each other.

It hurt.

All his life, he'd held himself away, closed himself off, unwilling to suffer the damn tortures that had changed Trask and made him less than whole. But somehow, though Dale had guarded himself before he'd even known what he was guarding against, she'd sneaked inside. She'd breached the defenses he'd built around his heart and she'd made herself a home there, safe and secure.

Until this. Until she'd seen the lies and the deceptions and the ugly, unhappy place he'd come from. Then, finally, she'd pulled away as he'd known all along she would. What they'd had was over. He felt its death right beside the pain. And even feeling it, he was unable to stop himself from crossing the room and sitting in the stiff chair beside her bed. He couldn't stop himself from sliding the safety of the hated shotgun, laying the weapon across his lap and groping for her hand in the darkness.

He needed to sit like this for a moment, and feel the peace she'd always brought to his soul. He needed to let his breathing match hers and his heartbeat slow until it kept pace with the pulse that surged just beneath his fingertips.

In the darkness, knowing he'd hear if anyone tried to sneak into the little room, Dale let his head fall back against the wall and closed his eyes. He stroked his thumb across the softest part of her wrist.

And fell asleep with the memory of her wrapped around his heart like a soft, warm, healing blanket.

IT WAS STILL DARK WHEN he felt the tug at his sleeve, but the darkness was broken now by gleams of gray light spearing between the plywood boards. Dale came awake with a jolt and grabbed for the shotgun before he realized the door was still closed.

The bolt was still on.

The tug came again.

"Excuse me, Unc' Dale? Have you seen my rock?"

He fumbled for the bedside lamp and clicked it on, only to find little Eddie, swaying on his feet, blinking owlishly into the yellow light less than a foot away from the loaded shotgun.

"Hey!" Dale shot to his feet and staggered with sudden light-headedness. He reached out a hand when Eddie stumbled backward in surprise. "Sorry, kid. Here." He plunked the boy in the chair. "Stay there. I'll be right back."

He used the bathroom and put the shotgun high atop the cheap medicine cabinet, way back where the kid couldn't reach. By the time he returned to the main room, Tansy was awake. He tried to steel himself against the desperate kick of his heart when her voice, low and husky with sleep, asked the little boy how he was feeling.

But his strength to resist her was failing.

"Okay," Eddie replied in a small voice. "Tired." He looked from Tansy to Dale and back. "Have you seen my rock? I had it with me before…at the river…" His lower lip trembled slightly. "It was in my pocket. I was gonna give it to Ma, and now I can't find it."

Foreboding streaked through Dale like lightning.

"Is this what you're looking for, honey? It fell out of your pocket when your pa brought you in." Tansy fished around in the pocket of her borrowed jeans and pulled out a rock.

A dull, ugly, purple rock.

Unease crystallized to certainty in that instant. Dale kept his tone level and his words even. "Can I see that?" He held out his hand, aware that he hadn't hidden his reaction from Tansy, who stared at him, curiosity and wariness battling for dominance in her eyes.

"What is it?" she asked, also careful to keep her voice nonthreatening in front of the small boy. "Dale? What is it?"

"It's probably nothing," he said, but he knew it was a lie. He dug into his pocket and pulled out his rock. Held the two up side by side in the sickly yellow light of the motel lamp.

They were identical in color and texture, though Dale's was slightly larger and had sharper edges. If he had to guess, he'd say the child's rock had been worn smooth by water.

His, on the other hand, had come from the source.

"Eddie, did you find this rock in the same river where you found the ring?" he asked quietly, aware of Tansy's quick flash of understanding.

The boy nodded, his eyes fastened on the two rocks. "Uh-huh. Where'd you get yours?"

"From my mother," Dale said quietly. "But I don't know where she found it." He felt Tansy's hand on his shoulder, and reached up to cover it with his own, just then needing the comfort more than he needed the distance. "Why don't we—"

A heavy fist pounded on the motel door. Dale shot to his feet, thinking of trip wires and a burning house. "Tansy, take Eddie into the bathroom with you. The shotgun is on top of the medicine cabinet."

"But Dale—"

"Just do it, please! I don't have time to argue."

Then he heard Trask's voice over the pounding. "Dale, Tansy, open up!"

"Damn it!" Dale yanked open the door and found Hazel, Trask and Mickey outside in the gray light of a cloudy midmorning. "You scared the—" he glanced back at Eddie's round eyes "—stuffing out of us." He stepped back into the room. "But I'm glad you're here. We have something to show you."

"So do we," Trask retorted. "In Unit 1." The older man grabbed Dale by the sleeve and tugged him outside. Tansy followed, and Mickey stayed behind in the room with his son.

Dale closed his fist over the dull purple rocks, which burned his skin, though they were cool and smooth. The stones were a link between the current outbreak and the past murders. But what did it mean?

Then Trask stopped outside a half-open door. Dale peered past him and cursed roundly.

Tansy peeked around them both and let out a low moan. "He's gone."

The motel room was identical to the others, save for the glaring absence of boards on the windows and the signs of a hasty exit. The bed was torn apart, the mattress slightly askew, as though Roberts had hidden something beneath it. There were no suitcases or signs that he was coming back. His cologne, fruity and vaguely feminine, hung in the air like a ghost.

Dale shook his head. "Where the hell could he go? There's a hurricane coming."

"Maybe, maybe not." Dale spun toward the new voice even as he recognized Churchill's cultured tones.

"What do you mean?"

"The storm has changed track." Churchill gestured at the sky, which was an unhealthy shade of yellow-gray. "They say it may miss us completely." He looked from one to the other of them. "Why? What have you discovered?"

Dale crossed his arms and felt the tension hammer at his temples. "Plenty."

They had discovered that the deaths were linked. Their prime suspect had disappeared while they were sleeping. What sort of investigators did that make them?

Tired ones, Dale admitted. Tired, frustrated investigators whose normal specialty was infected vectors and disease spread, not poisonings and purple rocks. He looked at Tansy, exhausted and beautiful, and his heart shuddered at what he'd gotten her into. He glanced at Trask and felt the familiar resentment, then at Hazel, who looked too old, too worn to be coping with a dying island. Finally, his eyes settled on Churchill, who had saved him so many years ago, when Dale's grief and teenage anger could so easily have taken him in a different direction.

These, Dale thought, were his connections. His family.

The thought warmed him.

It terrified him.

But rather than giving in to either of the emotions, he spread a level look among them and gestured to the room where Eddie waited with his father. "I think it's time we sat down and made a plan."

AFTER BRINGING CHURCHILL up to speed, Dale questioned Eddie about the rock. He knelt down to the boy's level, aware that Trask had a calming hand on the kid's shoulder.

Dale tried not to resent the gesture, knowing there was a time he would've given anything for just such kindness from his uncle. But that time was long past. He didn't need anything from Trask. Didn't need anything from anyone, except knowledge that would help him understand what had happened to his parents fifteen years earlier.

And what was happening now on Lobster Island.

"Eddie? Where did you get this rock?"

The kid's lower lip wobbled and he looked to his father for support. Mickey nodded. "Go ahead and tell him, son. Was it the same place you found the ring?"

"Yessir," Eddie whispered, staring at his bare feet as though he'd done something wrong. "I know you said not to go out looking by myself, but I 'membered something."

Dale leaned closer, aware of Tansy standing above him, aware of the twin rocks clutched in his fist. "What did you remember, Eddie?"

"I 'membered that the river was near the ghost tree. That was how I found it again."

"Do you know where this tree is?" Hazel quietly asked Trask. Since their arrival, the older couple had been quiet, speaking only to the others, not to each other. The tension between them added a subtle, angry layer to the uneasy atmosphere within the small room.

The older man nodded. "On the south claw, in the dense thickety area where most people don't go. Rumor says the tree was once used for a hanging. Not too many kids bother with it nowadays because the path is so overgrown."

"Teenagers used to go up there to neck," Dale observed, staring down at the rocks.

"Miranda and her boyfriend," Tansy said, and her voice shivered through Dale and left the fine hairs on his arms standing at attention. "Maybe they saw something there…"

"Like what?" Dale demanded. "It's just an old, ugly tree next to a river. What is there to see?"

"Maybe not a 'what,' but a 'who,'" Churchill murmured. Seated on the edge of the spare bed, his clothing and posture perfect, he could just as well have been presiding over a board meeting.

It didn't take the touch of embroidery at the cuffs and collar of his imported shirt for Dale to realize exactly who he'd been modeling himself after all these years.

And how badly he'd failed. Churchill was classy. Dale had merely pretended to be.

"You think they saw Roberts near the river?" Tansy asked. "Why would he be there?"

"It's the main source of fresh water for the island," Trask answered. "If it's true that the outbreak was a deliberate thing…"

Dale's guts froze as the implications sank in. "God," Tansy said, echoing his thoughts, "he could poison the entire island."

"But why?" Mickey asked.

Dale opened his hand and looked at the two ugly purple rocks. "The night she died, my mother told me she knew how she was going to pay for my college education. I didn't think much of it at the time, but lately I've been wondering. What if she found something here on the island? Something valuable?"

Galvanized by a sudden need to know, he strode to the bathroom, pulled down the shotgun and racked it hard enough to make the others flinch. "Come on. Outside."

A thick, age-softened concrete wall provided a safe backdrop, and Dale felt only a momentary twinge when he leaned down and placed his lucky rock on a brick beside the wall. When he'd retreated a safe distance and waved the others well back, he murmured, "Sorry, Mama." Then he aimed the shotgun in the general direction of the stone, slightly off center, and pulled the trigger.

The blast gouged a chunk out of the wall and shattered the brick into nasty slinging shards that the others ducked. Dale felt a piece kick off his shin, but he barely flinched. His attention was centered on the purple rock, which had bounded twenty feet away to lie, seemingly intact, in the middle of the motel parking lot.

"Damn it." He stalked over on stiff legs, aware of the worry in Tansy's eyes and the fact that she probably thought he'd flipped. Then again, maybe he had. That was the only reason he was considering the crazy plan that had come to him. They'd be safer hiding out in Churchill's mansion, drinking the last of the bottled water until help arrived. She'd be safer in the mansion, for sure.

But suddenly, he didn't think he could hide. The others were counting on their help. The *island* needed their help. So he stooped down and inspected the ugly purple rock. There was a long crack running through its center.

Dale reversed the shotgun and smashed it into the ground, butt first. When he pulled it away, the rock lay neatly halved. The broken facets were smooth and shiny, a deep royal purple that glowed with an inner light.

The center of the stone was shot through with a lightning bolt of yellow, a burst of color that Dale could imagine faceted and set, hanging from the graceful curve of Tansy's neck.

He glanced at her. "I think we've found our 'why.'"

She stepped closer and leaned down, and everything in Dale's body relaxed with her nearness and tensed up from the greed. Without any real thought, he picked up the two halves and handed one to her. He put the other in his pocket. When he stood, they were facing each other, barely a breath apart.

"We're heading upriver to find Roberts, aren't we?" she asked. Her body language told him in no uncertain terms that she would not be left behind, as did her addition of, "Partner."

But Dale had no intention of leaving her. Somewhere along the line, he'd gotten used to treating her as a lover and had forgotten about being her partner. She was the better, stronger half of their team. And this is what HFH doctors did.

They saved lives.

So he nodded and stuck out a hand. "Yes we are. Partner."

But when their hands gripped and held, and their eyes locked and a spark of connection arced between them, it was all he could do not to drag her into his arms and kiss her until none of it mattered anymore—not the past or the future, or the things they never seemed to get quite right between them.

And not the specter of the man he imagined waiting for them, high above the water on the deserted hill that made up the southern claw.

Chapter Ten

"I'm going with you, too." Trask's announcement was unexpected and not entirely welcome. Dale turned on his uncle, intending to tell him that he and Tansy would be better off traveling light and alone, as they had so many other times before. But Hazel beat him to it.

"The hell you are!" She glared at Trask, who recoiled in surprise. "We'll wait here until we're certain the storm has missed us. Then when help arrives from the mainland, we can turn this over to the authorities. There's no need for foolish heroics." Her voice climbed toward shrill on the last few words.

"But, Hazel—"

"No!" she snapped at him, her eyes welling with tears. "When will it be enough? Sue is dead. I don't know why you can't just accept it and move on."

Trask reached for her, his eyes dark and confused. She evaded his hands. "Don't bother, Trask. I've had enough of waiting for you. It's over, do you understand me? Over." Then, as suddenly as it had come, the fight seemed to drain out of her. She gave a shaky laugh and scrubbed both hands across her face. "Never mind. You're right."

Trask scowled helplessly. "Right about what?"

"It's up to us to find Roberts. He can't be allowed to poison the river."

If that was even his plan. They had nothing to go on besides their suspicion that the answers lay upriver.

"There is no *we* here," Dale said quickly. "Tansy and I are going because we're trained in this sort of thing." That was a stretch, but there was no way he was taking Hazel and Trask along. "Besides," he said, scrambling for a reason to leave them behind other than *You're too old,* or *I don't want anything to happen to you,* "Hazel needs to stay behind in case there are more poisonings."

She treated him to a withering glare. "You know as well as I do that there'll be no need for respirators if he hits the river." She widened her grimace to include Trask. "We're going along whether you like it or not. There's safety in numbers."

"She's right," Churchill said quietly, lifting his hand when Dale rounded on him. "You'll need someone to watch your back if he is up there."

"But the patients."

"There will be no new patients, Dale. You know it. And the few left alive here just need sleep. Mickey and I can watch over them." Churchill sighed. "I'd go up with you, but my knees just won't take it. Besides, don't you think Trask deserves to go?"

Because of Suzie. Dale hung his head, feeling the arguments slip away. All except one. "I don't want anyone hurt on account of me."

Trask lifted a tentative hand to Dale's shoulder. The weight was heavy and solid. Family. "It's not on account of you, boy. It's for the island."

Dale felt Tansy's eyes on him and met her questioning gaze when he nodded his head. "We go together, then."

As the four filed out of the motel room and into the yellow-gray light, Dale thought he heard Churchill murmur, "And may luck go with you."

Dale touched the broken stone in his pocket, heard it clink against his mother's engagement ring and wondered whether there was any such thing as luck on Lobster Island.

And if so, whether it had any use for him.

THEY PILED INTO TRASK'S jeep and drove down to the docks for supplies. There was no sharing seats on this trip. Tansy and Hazel sat pressed together on the tiny back bench while Dale and Trask manned the front. Conversation was nonexistent as Hazel and Trask brooded over their fight, Dale and Tansy over their plans.

Churchill claimed the storm had turned, but the clouds hung heavy and gray.

The air, though, remained motionless. Tansy felt the moisture in it cling to the insides of her nostrils and the back of her neck. She rubbed her arms and felt the fine hairs ripple as though lightning had struck nearby.

"Storm's coming," Trask grunted as he parked the jeep. "Churchill's weather folk are dead wrong about the hurricane turning. I'd bet a full catch she's headed straight at us."

As if in answer, a breeze tugged at Tansy's hair. It wasn't a refreshing wind, though. It was cold and wet and full of malice.

Dale's lips set as he considered the implications. "We can't turn back now."

"You're right," Tansy agreed. "Roberts has a solid head start on us. He could make it to the headwater before the storm."

Trask and Churchill had agreed that for Roberts to poison the island, he would have to follow the river upstream to the place where a larger flow branched into three smaller ones. Those three together fed the water supplies of the entire island.

Hazel gritted her teeth, visibly daring any of the others to suggest she stay in town with Mickey and Churchill. "Then let's get to it."

Tansy slid out of the jeep, onto to the deserted lobster dock. A shiver crawled down her back. The docks had looked barren before, when the *Churchill IV* had pulled her and Dale from the water and brought them ashore. Now, with the remaining boats either winched out of the battering surf or sent around to the other side of the island for safety, the dock moaned its emptiness.

Or maybe that was the wind.

"Tansy, you and Hazel look in the sheds for slickers and rope. Trask, you come with me. We'll need a machete or two, and shotgun shells if you have them." There was a fierce, bright light in Dale's eyes that made him look like the man Tansy had known in Tehru, and a hundred places since. The man she'd fallen in love with.

Action suited him, just as it suited her. She felt the siren's call of it thrum through her veins and pound just beneath her skin like tribal drums.

Like thunder. Or gunshots.

"You okay?" he asked, and she looked up to find him close. Too close. She could smell his familiar scent over the stink of the incoming storm, and wanted to kiss him. Wanted to drive herself into him and wrap him around her until there was nothing but them and the storm.

And of the future? There was no future beyond the incoming hurricane and the hunt they undertook. It was always this way for them in the field, when they took that first step away from the safe base hospital and out into the unknown. Here, they were finally in their element. And though they might not ever leave this island, or the river that beckoned with glittering gems and a madman's trail, Tansy had the wild urge to throw her head back and laugh into the threatening sky.

Instead, she looked straight at Dale, the man she'd loved despite everything, and nodded. "I'm great. Let's do this."

They found beacon-bright yellow rain jackets and pants hanging in the sorters' shed, and loaded up on rope and portables that might double as weapons. Canvas duffels were loaded with two machetes and a few assorted metal hooks with wickedly pointed ends. The doctor in Tansy shuddered at the thought of the barbs entering human flesh even as the survivor in her was glad for the protection.

And worried that they might need it.

On the drive to the southern claw, they swapped seat positions so she rode in the back with Dale, Hazel in the front with Trask. But still, there was little talk. It was difficult to converse over the engine and the rising wind.

Hurricane Harriet was on her way.

"We'll have to walk from here," Trask said, stopping the vehicle where the dirt road softened to sand. "We drive in much farther and the jeep's likely to sink with the rain."

They hiked down to the beach and walked along the heavy storm-tossed surf for nearly half a mile, passing churned up seaweed and dead and dying creatures. The charnel stench reminded Tansy of the cold room where the islanders had laid their dead.

When the storm passed, it would be time for burials and more tears.

When the storm passed...

They reached the river as the first fat drops of rain began to fall, and Tansy thought it was unnatural to hear water on all sides. The surf pounded behind her, the river gushed in front of her, and the rain beat a quickening tattoo all around, echoing hollowly on the yellow hood she pulled high and fastened across her throat.

The river was wide where it met the sea, running fast as though anticipating the rain and the wind. Tansy couldn't see any more of the glittering purple stones in the water or on its banks, but Eddie's rock had been a devious gray until it was held up to the sunlight. Only then had it shown its purple core.

She touched the shard of rock in her pocket and winced when a sharp edge pricked her finger.

"This way," Trask called over the symphony of water. He waved towards the thick wall of trees that verged the beach near this lonely, unused part of the island. "There used to be a path up to the headwater, back when I was a boy."

When he turned away, Tansy heard Dale's voice beside her. "I don't know if I would have found this place without him." The words echoed oddly through the rain hood.

Hating the way it narrowed her vision and obscured her hearing, she pushed the hood back off her head, noting that Dale had done the same. "What?"

"Trask," he repeated. "I think we were right to bring him."

Tansy watched the older man scramble up the shifting beach, towards the trees, with Hazel following doggedly in his wake. Their bright yellow raincoats glowed in the storm light, and the forest looked dank and dark, wreathed in an oily mist that would cling and slip rather than hide. She shivered with quick foreboding.

The brief burst of euphoria she'd felt at the prospect of one last field adventure with Dale faded, leaving behind the knowledge that this was no simple trek through a rainforest to an ailing village. No, this was a manhunt, pure and simple, with a posse of four, a single shotgun and a short dozen shells.

She glanced up at Dale and saw her own reservations written in his cool blue eyes. She longed to kiss him, to touch him, to reassure him that she was there for him, would always be there for him. But he didn't want that. Didn't want her.

Didn't want them.

So she took a deep breath and found a brave smile. "Hazel and Trask are fine. I'm not so sure about this rain gear, though."

"It's designed to show up against the water when a lobsterman goes overboard." Dale looked toward the trees, where the others glowed like neon. "Let's keep them on for now and ditch them about halfway up. Roberts has a good head start, and he won't be expecting pursuit, so we should be safe until then."

"Hoy there!" came Trask's shout from up the beach. "We've found the path."

But when they reached it, the so-called path seemed even more densely wooded than the stunted beach forest around them. In theory, the trail followed the wide river from the verge of the sand and sawgrass, up a rocky hill to the tall hump of the southern claw. Most of the settlements on the island, along with the dock and the airstrip, stretched along the creature's tail and northern claw, leaving the southern claw bare. Though Tansy knew "civilization" was no more than three or four miles away, the distance felt much greater than that.

She held out a hand to stop Dale when he would have followed his uncle right away. "Are you sure this is the best plan? Something feels wrong to me."

He shook her off. "We don't have a choice, Tansy. The islanders need us."

He hadn't answered her question, which was all the reply she needed. He felt it, too. But she could tell from the frenetic glint in Dale's eyes and from Trask's wild, driven motions as he hacked away at the underbrush and forced a path where one used to be, that the men weren't simply bent on saving the island.

They were looking for revenge.

The first band of rain passed, and in the capricious way of storm skies, the clouds parted to let a finger of sunlight break through. Tansy lifted her face into the weak warmth for a moment. Then she looked into the jagged maw Trask had carved out of the tangled growth. Dark and forbidding, it oozed a wet mist that smelled like rotting vegetation. Or worse.

"I'm not sure this is such a good idea anymore," she murmured to herself. "The storm hasn't turned and we have one shotgun among the four of us. Why are we doing this again?"

"Because we love them," Hazel answered unexpectedly. The middle-aged doctor stepped up beside Tansy and brushed her hood back as they watched Trask and Dale hack their way into the dark, stinking undergrowth. "And because they need us."

"Dale doesn't need anyone," Tansy answered, aware of a simmering layer of resentment.

Hazel laughed softly. "That's what he wants you to believe, child. But I've never seen anyone need another human being the way Dale needs you. His eyes follow you when you're not looking. He leans on you, and you don't even notice it."

Grunts of exertion, the thwack of machetes and the rustles of brush being dragged aside punctuated the men's progress, but on the beach, Tansy felt that wan ray of sunlight touch her face again.

Or maybe it was hope.

"Do you think so?" she asked quietly.

Hazel shot her a glance. "I know so. But it's not enough." The stern warning in her voice was enough to kill the quick tremble of optimism struggling to life in Tansy's heart. Belatedly, she remembered her parents.

Her father had needed her mother to organize his dinner parties and charm his clients' wives. He'd needed her to keep the household running smoothly and see to the raising of their only daughter. He'd needed her.

But it hadn't been enough.

She stared at her toes. "I know."

"You need to decide what you need from him, and tell him so." Hazel touched Tansy's elbow and gestured her towards the raw, bleeding pathway the men had sliced for them. Her voice dropped toward bitter. "Then you need to be prepared to walk away if he can't give it to you."

Tansy thought of Trask and Hazel, who each glanced over when they thought the other wasn't paying attention. Though she hadn't seen the expression on Dale's face, ever, Tansy recognized it from her mother's face. From her own. Need. Stark longing. A wish.

Then she thought of the thing keeping Trask and Hazel apart—a man's love for his dead wife, and his inability to say goodbye without knowing the truth. And she realized there was another reason for Dale and Trask to enter that weeping, oozing hole in the forest.

They needed to lay the dead to rest.

"Come on, then. Let's do this." She touched Hazel's arm and they walked along the river to the place where a path had once run. With a shudder of foreboding, Tansy realized that the stumps of the slashed brambles were too even, too regularly spaced to be natural. The path had been covered up on purpose, many years ago. But where did it lead?

She touched the broken rock in her pocket. It made her think the trail might lead to a vein of precious stones crumbling from a hillside far above the riverbank, where pieces washed down with the rains now and then. And islanders unlucky enough to find them were *lost at sea*.

If that was the case, then someone on the island must be involved. Roberts was a newcomer. The brambles, and Lobster Island's reputation, had been sown years ago. As had the legend of a ghost in Dale's old house. Perhaps it wasn't a ghost then, but a very human search for the rock Dale had carried all these years.

But who could it be? Tansy thought of the islanders she'd met—poor, honest folk who loved their families and their island, even when it gave them back nothing but heartache. As she walked along the path, she realized she already had her answer.

Roberts would know. He would know who controlled the gems, and who had hired him to buy the island.

He might even know where the graves were.

Ripe male curses and the snick of metal on brush sounded up ahead, though Tansy couldn't see the men through the nasty fog rising from the forest floor. The brief ray of sunlight winked out, and the world was plunged back into the gray of the oncoming storm. She shivered slightly and forged on.

Scanning the ground for the best place to step foot, she noticed a small stone to one side. It might have been purple, though it was hard to tell in the stormy half light.

"Hey, I think I've got another one of the rocks!" She bent down beneath an overhanging limb and stepped off the path, reaching for the unassuming-looking lump.

Without warning, the ground gave way beneath her leading foot. "Aah!" She jerked back, trying to keep her balance, and banged her head against the low-slung branch.

Hazel yelled, "Trask! Dale! Help!"

And Tansy fell.

DALE TURNED BACK AT HAZEL'S cry. His gut clenched when he realized they couldn't see the women through the mist. He ran towards them, terror slamming in his ears. He saw only a single figure in the mist where two had been.

And his heart stopped.

"Tansy!" He charged to the place where she'd disappeared, and skidded to a halt at the edge of a crumbling void that had been disguised by a light mat of twigs, dirt and leaves. "It's a damn pit trap!"

There was so little light filtering through the low canopy that he couldn't see the bottom. Couldn't see Tansy. His heart started to beat again, but in an erratic gallop that seemed to say *Too late, too late, too late.*

"Tansy!" he called, "Tansy, honey, can you hear me?"

Trask shouldered Hazel aside, away from the jagged edge of the pit, and the three leaned down, peered through the darkness and saw…nothing.

Dale was taking a breath to yell again when he heard a rustle from the pit. Then Tansy's voice.

"Dale. I'm fine. Keep away from the edge. I don't think it's too stable." She was breathing hard, but her voice was strong, and he felt such a surge of relief and twisting guilt that he closed his eyes momentarily against the power of it. Against the power she held over him.

"Thank you, God," Hazel breathed, and the sentiment expressed everything that was in Dale's heart but would never be said.

"Can you shine one of the lights down here?" Tansy called up. "I'm wedged against something."

The lights. Of course. Dale reached into the pocket of his slicker for one of the flashlights they'd picked up at the dock. He aimed it into the hole and snapped it on.

His mouth dried to dust.

The pit was perhaps ten feet deep, and rough-sided. Tansy lay at the bottom, flat up against one wall. She was wedged, all right.

By a thick, sharpened stick.

"Huh." Trask blew out a breath and rocked back on his heels.

Dale felt a flash of irritation at his uncle's characteristic emotionlessness. If there was ever a time in his life that he wanted to panic, it was now. But he couldn't. Tansy needed him.

"Dale?" Her muffled voice carried upwards, sounding so much farther away than she really was. "Is it like the ones we saw in Africa?" With her face pressed against the dirt, she couldn't see that the pit was lined with thirty or so three-foot-long spikes. But she'd reached a hand back to touch the one that held her in place. The knowledge was in her voice, as was the fear.

"Yeah, it's like Africa," Dale said, unable to think of a reason to lie. They'd saved a village elder, and much of the village, from a rare pulmonary disease. The healthy men had hunted in celebration of the elder's recovery, and Dale and Tansy had been given the dubious honor of watching their dinner skewered to death in a pit not unlike this one.

Dale tried to banish the memory of the blood, and armor himself against the knowledge that he'd almost lost Tansy just now. "Hang on," he said inanely, aware that his voice cracked on the second word. "I'm coming down there."

He shushed the chorus of protests with a quick gesture. "You're not strong enough to boost her up if she's hurt," he said to Hazel. He turned to Trask. "And I'm trusting you to haul me out."

Something shifted in the older man's eyes, an emotion hidden beneath so many layers it almost couldn't find its way out. Dale held his hand out for a shake, and somehow the shake became an embrace.

For a brief moment, Dale was seventeen again. No longer a boy, not quite a man, he'd stood beside the empty graves and wished for a hug. Now, standing beside the pit that could have been Tansy's grave, he realized something.

Fifteen years later wasn't too late, after all.

"Of course, boy." Trask turned away and cleared his throat as he pulled one of the thick, fishy ropes from the bags they'd hauled with them.

Dale handed the shotgun to Hazel. "Here, keep an eye on this for me, will you?"

An islander to the core, she said nothing, merely accepting the weapon with a nod.

With Trask counterweighting the rope, Dale slid down the crumbling side of the pit, flashlight clamped between his teeth. The moist dirt was cool and faintly slimy to the touch, and a shower of small rocks cascaded down on his head every time Trask's feet shifted.

"Dale? Watch out for the spikes."

He grinned around the flashlight at Tansy's unnecessary caution, but understood her need to say something. Anything.

His feet touched bottom more quickly than he might have imagined, and he let go of the rope that had slowed his descent. Above, Trask cursed in relief. The lobsterman was tough as nails, but deadweight was deadweight.

"I'm here, Tans." Dale didn't waste time with a survey of their surroundings. Instead, he knelt, and ran quick, testing fingers over her.

"I said I'm fine," she snapped as though she didn't want him touching her, but he passed it off as stress and maybe a bit of shock.

"I just want to make sure there aren't any hidden injuries, Tans." He spoke soothingly, as he might to a patient, and was startled when she slapped at him with her free hand.

"Just get me out of here, okay? I think I'm lying on…something." Her voice tailed up at the end of the sentence. When she began to struggle in earnest, Dale abandoned proper procedure and helped lever her up and aside, freeing her left arm where it had been pinned beneath her, and sliding her away from the unyielding spike.

"You're okay. I've got you." He wasn't sure which one of them needed it more, but he dragged her into his arms and held on tight, heedless of the flashlight dropping to the floor of the pit. "I've got you."

She burrowed in tight and hung on. He wondered if she could feel his heart beating fast and furious. Part of him hoped she couldn't.

"You two okay down there?" A flashlight beam from above caught them for a few seconds, then discreetly slid away. Trask muttered, "Oh, sorry."

But it was enough to interrupt the moment. Dale released Tansy, waiting a moment to make sure she was solid on her feet, then called up to Trask, "Stand by on the rope. Let's get her out of here."

With a heave and an indelicate boost, Dale helped Tansy scramble up the side of the pit. Chunks of wormy dirt broke free as she gained the outside.

Suddenly alone in the damp darkness, he bent down and scooped up the flashlight, which had fallen near where she had been trapped. The beam glinted off something other than dirt. Dale froze.

I think I'm lying on...something. And she had been, though not the bones that he had briefly feared.

No, it wasn't a skeleton. But it was evidence that they weren't the first to visit the bottom of the pit. Splinters of rotted wood suggested that spikes had been shattered and replaced. And a cheap plastic watch lay broken, abandoned beside a corroded piece of jewelry.

"You ready?" Trask called down from above.

Dale flashed his light quickly around the pit, which was maybe ten feet square. Spikes and dirt. No other signs of violence, which in a way made the evidence all the spookier. He bent and picked up the watch and what turned out to be a friendship locket, of the sort island high school boys might give to their sweethearts when the couple agreed to go steady.

"Ready." Past ready, Dale thought, as the rope snaked back down to the bottom of the pit. "Get me the hell out of here."

Though it was dark and drizzly, and the wind had sprung back up after their brief respite, he felt a blast of warmth as he emerged from the pit trap back onto the ground level of Lobster Island. Maybe it was being out of that black, deathly pit, he thought.

Or maybe it was the sight of Tansy, Trask and Hazel waiting for him.

Chapter Eleven

They gathered near the pit trap with their backs to the jagged hole, not ready to move on, but not wanting to stare into the obscene thing.

"Was it Roberts, do you think?" Hazel asked. Her eyes were stark and worried. She held the shotgun at the ready as though fearing the woods were alive with enemies.

As well they might be, Tansy thought.

Dale shook his head. "No, I think that's been there a long time, longer than Roberts has been on the island. And I'm worried that it's not the only one. Someone doesn't want us on this path, that much is clear." He glanced down at the cheap necklace and the broken watch he'd found at the bottom of the hole, and took a deep breath before his eyes found Tansy's. "I want you and Hazel to go back down to the jeep and wait for us. You'll be dry there, and she has the gun, so you'll be safe, too."

Though part of her wanted to run screaming, Tansy glared at Dale and wished the ground would open up and swallow him whole. Then she hugged herself and shuddered, realizing she'd never wish that on anyone ever again, having experienced it first-hand. Those first few moments, when she'd been trapped in the cold, oily blackness had been bad. Realizing she could easily have been killed was worse. But understanding that someone had laid the trap beside the old pathway and baited it with a chunk of the purple rock?

That was downright gruesome.

Still, she clenched her jaw and shook her head. "I'm not going back without you. We're a team."

A team. That was all, because Hazel was right. It wasn't about what Dale would or wouldn't take from her anymore. It was about what he could give her.

What she deserved.

Dale bared his teeth in a feral expression so far removed from Dr. Dale Metcalf, M.D., that she backed up a step. "Damn it! Why can't you be sensible and go wait in the car? This doesn't have anything to do with you, don't you get that?"

Tansy flinched but stood firm. She thought she caught a ghost of desperation in his expression, but it might have been wishful thinking. She would give him this before they said goodbye. She'd see him through this quest for his parents, this search for his past, then she'd go, knowing she had done her very best.

But also knowing that she'd accepted defeat before she lost her self-respect.

"I'm. Not. Leaving." She glared up at him. "Got it?"

He didn't answer. He stared down at her, breathing heavily, his eyes darkening almost to midnight.

In that instant, she thought he might kiss her and every traitorous, womanly fiber in her body yearned for the contact, yearned for the warmth amidst the cold and the calm amidst the storm. They swayed ever so slightly toward each other, compelled by a force greater than the wind.

"Just kiss her and let's move on," Trask demanded from behind them, "We've got maybe two hours before the storm hits for real." He punctuated the complaint with an *oof* that Tansy figured came from an elbow planted in his ribs.

But the interruption was for the best, she knew. She stepped away from Dale and shook her head. "Neither Hazel nor I are going back to the car. We're all going to hike up to the headwater and stop Roberts. If we're lucky, we'll find the source of the stones—" she touched her pocket "—and maybe…"

The graves. They all thought it, but not one of them could say the words. The wind chose that moment to howl through the trees like the tortured damned and Tansy flinched.

"Fine." Dale cursed. "Have it your way." He finally backed off and nodded, though his eyes stayed that deep, intimidating color they took on when he was really upset.

Or really turned on. The memory brought frantic blood chasing through Tansy's body, remembering how it had been between them. And though it was unwise and probably destructive, she let the memory come and drive away the feeling of damp, rotting earth and the smell of old blood and new fear.

At least it made her feel warmer, for a little while.

WHEN THEY REACHED the headwater, it was almost anticlimactic. There was no sign of Roberts, nor any evidence that he'd been there. There was nobody to claim the broken watch and the locket. Though Trask had been unable to identify the items, his mention of missing boat crews had started Dale wondering.

What if fishing off Lobster Island wasn't as dangerous as the numbers suggested?

What if it was living *on* Lobster Island that killed people?

"Now what?" Standing at his shoulder, Tansy asked the question for all of them. The woods thinned at the edge of the river, allowing the gray daylight to filter through, along with more of the rain and the wind.

Harriet, it seemed, was in a hurry to reach Lobster Island, after all.

"I don't know." Damn it. He'd been so sure this was the key. They would reach the headwater, find Roberts and he would lead them to…what? Dale wasn't even sure anymore whether he was looking for the source of the pseudo-PSP or the bodies of his parents.

Part of him feared he would find both.

"Are we sure this is the right place?" Hazel asked, joining them at the water's edge.

Trask nodded. "Yeah. But I don't see any of the stones."

The older man had been growing increasingly more agitated as the trek wore on. Dale understood, as he was feeling it, too. There was a growing sense of danger coming from all directions, along with the confusion that came from not knowing enough.

Tansy often fretted because she wanted to know more, always more. Before, he'd found it irritating, an invasion.

Now, he understood how she felt.

"I see one!" Hazel's excited shout yanked their attention upstream, to where she hung off an overreaching limb, straining toward the water. "I've found one of the rocks!"

Trask cursed and started toward her at a run. "Damn it, Hazel, be quiet and get back! You're going to—"

Fall in.

The branch broke and Hazel overbalanced with a cry. She splashed ungracefully into the waist-deep water, surfaced once, and disappeared.

"The slicker!" Dale yelled to the running Trask. "Her slicker's filled with water." Damn it, he knew he should've left the things behind. But turning them inside out and rubbing them with dirt had camouflaged the bright colors enough that he'd thought it safe to keep them on in the cold, cutting wind.

Now, it seemed that he'd been wrong.

"No kidding," snapped the veteran lobsterman.

He tore off his own jacket and plunged into the river after Hazel.

He stumbled and went under almost immediately. Dale was halfway out of his own jacket when he saw his uncle surge back up, clutching Hazel around her torso.

Both of them were coughing and spluttering, but unhurt when they dragged themselves ashore.

"God, are you okay?" Dale knew his question was inane, but didn't know how to articulate the things he was feeling.

Feelings were Tansy's department.

"Well, I won't worry about getting wet from the rain anymore." Huddled against Trask's solid bulk, Hazel attempted a smile through lips that were already beginning to tremble from the cold. "I feel stupid as hell, though. I don't know what I was thinking."

"Hush," Trask ordered. "You're about the least stupid person I've ever met."

As a declaration of undying love, Dale figured it left a bit to be desired, but Hazel glowed at the compliment.

"Dale, they're going to freeze in about five minutes," Tansy murmured, nudging him in the side. "Damp is one thing, soaking wet is another."

He nodded. "Yeah." Raising his voice over the freshening wind, he said, "Go back down, both of you. You'll catch your deaths if you stay up here."

The words seemed oddly prophetic.

"I'm fine," Trask declared, standing up and

staunchly wringing out the tails of his shirt. "That's my wife we're searching for. I want to stay."

Hazel closed her eyes, and a look of exquisite pain washed across her features.

Tansy faced Trask, hands on hips, crowding into his personal space with her jaw thrust out and her eyes blazing. "Your wife is dead." When Trask fell back a step, Tansy advanced. "Hazel is here, not Suzie. Hazel. She needs you, Trask, and you're damn well going to get your head out of your past and give her what she needs, got it?"

"Tansy, this isn't necessary," Hazel said quietly, climbing to her feet. "Let him go. He needs to find his wife, and Roberts must be stopped. I'll walk back down and lock myself in the jeep. Take this, you'll need it." She handed the shotgun to Tansy.

With as much dignity as she could muster, bedraggled and sopping wet, the island's doctor turned and stomped back down the path, squishing as she went.

The others stood motionless for a moment. Dale stared at Hazel's retreating back, wondering what had just happened and feeling somehow guilty for it. Tansy stared at Trask, jaw clenched, fury in her eye.

Finally, Trask cursed and strode after Hazel, seeming more powerful soaking wet rather than less. At the verge of the heavy growth, he turned back. "Take care of yourself, boy." Dale felt the punch of his uncle's concern and felt a small, scared wish that it hadn't taken fifteen years for him to return to the island. Then Trask jerked his chin toward Tansy. "And take care of her, you hear?"

And that small, scared boy's wish coalesced into a man's determination. Nothing was going to harm his Tansy. Nothing.

He locked his jaw and nodded once. "I will."

When Trask and Hazel had been swallowed up in the sulky forest mist, Dale turned to Tansy. "Think the gun is any good now that it's been in the river?"

"I don't know." She handed it to him, then opened her palm and held it up. Dull purple glittered, reflecting the gray light off broken amethyst facets. "She gave me this, as well. She was right, she'd found one of the stones."

As though her words had unlocked the secret, a breath of warmer air blew across them, sweeping aside the rain and the wind. A gap in the clouds allowed the sun to struggle through in a single spotlight-beam of radiance that lit a cliff face across the river upstream of them. Tansy gasped and grabbed Dale's sleeve, but it was unnecessary.

He saw it. A glitter of purple fire cascading down from the dark, gaping mouth of a cave. He cursed under his breath as the knowledge washed over him, and the memory of Hazel's words. *Curtis was incoherent by then...kept rambling on about lightning bolts and Ali Baba's cave.*

The teenagers, Dale's parents and God only knew how many others in between had been murdered to protect the location of the cave. And if they didn't get out of here, fast, he and Tansy would be next.

"COME ON. We've found the stones and missed Roberts. Let's head back and regroup."

Tansy braced her feet in the mud as the feeble sunlight guttered and died. "Shouldn't we investigate the cave?"

Dale's face darkened and the sky rumbled behind him. "Absolutely. Positively. Not. Let's go."

She allowed him to tug her down the path they'd cut through the bracken, but she took one long look back over her shoulder. The gray sky cast no sparkles on the runoff, but she'd seen them. The gems drew her just as surely as the cave repelled her. Like the forest, it seemed old and evil. Waiting.

She shivered as the rain began again and a fat drop slid down the back of her neck. Trying to hurry, she scrambled along the sloppy track behind Dale, feeling the mud suck at her boots with every step. Feeling as though something dark and evil was chasing them down to the beach.

"Faster!" she shouted to Dale, sensing the storm building more violently than she could have imagined, knowing that the hurricane had finally arrived. "We've got to get down to the— Aah!" The mud gave way beneath her right foot and she fell to the side. Kept falling as her leg plunged through into emptiness. "Dale!"

"Damn!" He grabbed her arm and yanked her

back to solid ground. They stared at the hole, breathing heavily. He cursed. "Another pit trap."

By poking the ground before they stepped on it, the group had avoided two more of the booby traps along the way. They'd missed this one, which was just to the side of the path they'd cut.

His fingers gentled on her arm, though he didn't move away. Tansy's urgency of a moment ago shifted, becoming a new, warmer urgency. One she didn't trust.

"Come on, we need to get moving," she called over the rising wind, and the rattling sound of raindrops hitting their yellow rubberized slickers like drumbeats.

But Dale didn't move. He stayed there, fingers now caressing her arm as he stared down at her with unreadable emotions crowding his eyes.

Dale? Emotions? Confusion pricked deep in Tansy's chest. But before she could ask, he said, "I am so sorry I got you into this, Tans. So damn sorry."

And like a punch in the gut, she finally understood that part of his need to drive her away came not from the fact that he wanted her out of his life, but because he was afraid for her. He wanted her safe.

He cared.

But just as she was thinking it was too little, too late that she had learned her worth on Lobster Island and she deserved better than scraps of his heart, he kissed her.

And all other thoughts fled.

His taste, familiar yet not, exploded across her lips and tongue like the flash of lightning that glowed red through her closed eyelids. Thunder chased on the heels of its lightning, but she could barely hear it over the pounding of blood in her ears as Dale crowded close to her.

Dale, her mind whimpered as her body flared to life. *Dale.*

Everything was cool and wet—from the rain, from the air. Except for their mouths. The heat lay there, in the slippery junction of bodies otherwise held apart by rubber rain suits and history.

She sank, almost unwillingly, deeper into the kiss when he slanted his mouth across hers, seeking more. Always more. This was the one place he never held back from her.

Straining closer to him, she felt cold, wet clothing stick to suddenly heated places with a torturous friction. When the rain cascaded down on them amidst a mutter of thunder, neither of them moved. The touch of their lips heated the rain to a warm shower, and the contrast of hot and cold was maddening.

Like the man himself.

Remembering her vow, and her worth, Tansy eased away from Dale with real regret. He stared down at her, eyes huge and dark, then shook himself, face suddenly fierce. "What the hell are we doing?"

Tansy ignored the twinge of hurt. Hot and cold. That was Dale. "We're getting out of here," she yelled over the wind, then jumped and shrieked when there was a strange *zzzzzt* sound and the twisted tree beside her jerked and toppled over. "Lightning!"

"Hell!" Dale knocked her down and covered her with his body as two other trees were cut down with wet-sounding thwacks from invisible machetes. "It's not lightning. He's shooting at us!"

"He's what? Who?" Tansy yelled over the wind and the rain and a scattering of wild shots, unable to believe this was actually happening to them. They were being *shot* at, for God's sake.

"Roberts," Dale yelled back, keeping his head below the level of the knee-high leafy ground cover. "We found him. Or he found us. Come on!" He bellied backward off the path, staying low and moving fast.

Tansy followed, expecting at any moment to feel the heavy thud of impact, feel the delayed burn she imagined would come with a bullet wound. Her heart hammered in her ears, or maybe that was the ever-nearing thunder and the voice of Harriet as the hurricane descended upon Lobster Island.

They huddled behind a larger tree at the edge of the path and Dale peered around it. He held a hand back. "Give me the gun!" he yelled over the storm and the river's rush.

She passed it to him. "It's wet." There was no telling whether it would fire now. But it was their only hope.

"It had better," Dale called back, confirming her thoughts. "He's over there, between those two big rocks."

Tansy risked a look, figuring from the brief lull in the firing that Roberts must be reloading. She saw the rocks but not the man. "Are you sure?"

"Trust me." He clasped her shoulder in a brief squeeze, so the two words took on much more meaning. Then he let his hand drop and jerked his head back toward the cave. "When I say the word, I want you to run for the cave, got it? I'll cover you."

A bullet smacked into the tree beside Tansy's hand and she jumped back, feeling the sting in her fingers. "Dale, wait! I…"

"It's our only chance, Tans. We're sitting ducks out here, and the storm is only going to get worse. We've got to get across that river and up to the cave. It looks dry and we can defend it. I'll be right behind you. I promise." He gave her a not-too-gentle shove. "Now, go!"

Lightning flickered above them, and in its flash Tansy noticed something new in his eyes, though she couldn't have said exactly what it was.

Without another word, she turned and ran for the cave, trusting Dale to guard her back.

Gunfire erupted from the rocks on the other side of the path, quickly answered by the shotgun's deep-bellied roar. Thank God it had fired.

Tansy felt the mud give beneath her borrowed shoes and lunged forward, narrowly avoiding another pit trap. A bullet sang above her, in the place where her head had been just moments before.

The shotgun blasted again, sounding farther away,

and Tansy cursed at the knowledge that Dale was backing down the hill, endangering himself as he tried to buy her more time. "Damn it, Dale. Come on!" she muttered in between gasps as she gained the gritty shore of the river and fixed her eyes on the cave mouth high above the opposite side. An incongruous thread of white mist, maybe steam, bled from the tip of the cracked mouth. She had no fear of small spaces, but this cave, like the opening the men had hacked into the forest, seemed to be waiting for something. It seemed almost…alive.

She heard running footsteps behind her and spun to find Dale nearly on top of her. "Come on, sweetheart. Time to go!"

That was when she knew she was never coming out of the rabbit hole. Dale Metcalf had called her sweetheart.

"Did you get Roberts?"

His lack of a reply was answer enough, as was the ready hold he kept on the shotgun. They'd started the trip with twelve rounds. She'd counted ten blasts. That left them with two waterlogged shells.

Tansy gritted her teeth. "Let's go, then."

Hands linked, they waded into the water with Dale upstream so the force of the river would break around him. She gasped at the first shock. She'd thought herself cold and wet before. She'd been wrong.

The wind tore at them, howling through the shallow canyon like fury and beating against her until she thought it might be easier just to collapse into the river and let it sweep her away.

"Come on, damn you. Don't quit now." Dale dragged her a few steps closer to the far shore, which seemed a mile away. Her legs were numb and heavy. Her feet could have belonged to someone else. "Don't you dare quit on me!"

She took another step. Another. And the riverbed disappeared beneath her.

At her cry, Dale braced himself as best he could on the slippery rocks beneath the water and held tight to her hand. "Come on, you can do it!"

He couldn't drop the shotgun to save her. It was all they had. He'd left his duffel back by the bullet-riddled tree. Ropes and machetes would do them no good if they didn't make it to the cave.

"Dale!" Eyes wide with fright, lips blue with cold, she struggled back to her feet, hauling on his hand until he thought his shoulder might pop. She set her lips. "I'm fine. Let's go."

God, she was tough. Together, they trudged across the river. Inch by inch. Step by step. There was no sign of Roberts. Maybe he'd winged the man with one of his shots. Dale could only hope, because he was down to his last shell, having dropped one in his mad, zigzagging dash to the river. The force of the current dragged at his legs and the howling wind dragged at his body, but he did his best to shield Tansy from both. Slipping, stumbling, they hauled each other out of the water to the base of a steep incline. A crude flight of steps was hacked into the hillside.

"Wait." Tansy held him back. "The pit traps."

Dale froze and cursed himself for being stupid. The path to the river had been booby-trapped. Why not this one? "Do you see another way up?" The wind ripped the words from his mouth, but he barely felt the gale's brutal force anymore. His face was numb, and his hands and feet. They needed to get inside, out of the wind and the rain, out of the open.

He felt eyes on the back of his neck and glanced again at the dark forest on the other side of the river. Was that movement? Or just the bowing and swaying of the strange, twisted trees? Where the hell was Roberts?

"This way." Tansy scrambled up a narrower, faintly marked trail, testing each step and watching the ground carefully. "It seems okay."

Dale followed, keeping watch behind them. But even so, he couldn't help noticing the slick cling of wet cloth to her body as she worked her way up the slope. The surge of lust was familiar, yet spiked with something new. Desperation.

She stopped at the cave mouth and waved him forward, the caution in her eyes bringing a new fear. What if Roberts had an accomplice? What if someone was waiting for them in the cave?

Zzzzzzt. Crack! The bullet smacked into the rock wall beside Dale's shoulder, and suddenly there was no time to worry about what waited for them inside the cave, because a tall figure in a long, dark green raincoat was wading determinedly across the river toward them.

Roberts.

"Get in the cave!" Dale yelled, shoving her inside. He had to yell, because the wind suddenly doubled in intensity, wailing and gnashing at the island, whipping the river to whitecaps that swirled around Roberts's legs, then his waist.

The raincoated figure staggered and dropped to one knee in the rushing water, leaving Dale to wonder whether he'd wounded the man already. Then he decided he didn't care. It was Roberts or them, and Dale had promised to keep Tansy safe. He was going to get her off the island or die trying.

Calmly, he lifted the shotgun and fired into the wind, trusting Hurricane Harriet to send the pellets back into the river. The blast was quiet in comparison to the sound of the storm, which blotted out any cry from the man below. The figure simply jerked, folded over and fell into the rushing, white-flecked water.

In moments, the dark green raincoat slipped around a bend in the river and was gone.

It took longer for Dale's system to level, and for the rough, ready rage to subside. Then he waited another minute, thinking the feeling of vindication should come next.

But it didn't. In its place lingered a vague disquiet and a growing, numbing cold where the wind and the rain bit down to his skin.

"Dale? Are you okay?" Then Tansy was at his side, and the cold didn't seem so bad anymore. But the adrenaline and the rage remained, tempered now to something that felt less like anger and more like heat. She touched his arm, igniting a thousand pin-prick fires. "There doesn't seem to be anyone else in the cave." She was silent for a moment, then asked, "Do you think he had a chance to dump the toxin in the river?"

"I don't know." Lightning flashed and thunder grumbled. The sky closed in for good, and almost all of the yellow-gray light was extinguished as though it had been sucked into the clouds. "I guess we'll have to trust Hazel, Trask and Churchill to keep the is-landers away from their taps until the storm passes."

Trust. It was a new concept for him, yet it seemed to fit well here, in this place that felt like the end of the earth.

"Come inside," she urged, tugging him toward the cave. "You're freezing."

They both were. Tansy's lips were blue, and Dale's fingers, nose and toes were numb. Now that Roberts was gone, they needed to concentrate on practical matters like getting warm.

Feeling as though he was taking a monumental step, Dale set one foot inside the cave. The wind pushed him with a gentle hand and he stepped an-other foot inside. And waited.

But there were no ghosts waiting for him. Only Tansy.

And she was everything.

The floor of the cave was covered with coarse, faintly purple sand. Hundreds of boot tracks pock-marked the surface, beginning four or five feet inside the cave as though the last big storm had washed away part of the humans' passing.

A few feet past the boot marks, the dim outside light failed and the cave, about ten feet across at that point, faded to inky black. Resigned to the sight he feared would greet him, Dale reached into his pocket and pulled out the sadly abused waterproof flashlight he'd borrowed from the sorting shed.

He flicked on the light and panned it across the cave, empty shotgun at the ready, just in case.

Then the light faltered.

The gun sagged.

And Tansy gasped.

It was beautiful. The flashlight's feeble yellow glow was picked up and thrown back at them from a hundred thousand facets. Purple-black. A slash of orangey yellow. Deep, throbbing green.

"God," Dale breathed, the word coming from deep in his gut. The walls of the arched cavern were an artist's palette, the stalactites hanging from the ceiling, spears of pure color.

"This is why they died," Tansy breathed at his shoulder, "so nobody would find this place."

She gestured, and Dale followed her gaze to the far wall, where tool marks and shattered crystal marked crude mining efforts. Dale felt his heart squeeze in his chest. Greed. It all came back to greed. "Yeah."

Almost unable to bear the sight of a natural wonder perverted to man's grand design, he doused the flashlight, once again becoming aware of the chill. The wind. Tansy's shivers. His own.

"Come on," he urged. "Let's see where the steam is coming from." Logically, it had to be hotter than the outside air, to create that thin track of white that wound around the jagged ceiling.

It wasn't until they'd crept halfway across the immediate cavern that Dale realized he could see shapes in the darkness, even though the flashlight was off.

"There's light up ahead," Tansy murmured, a quiver in her voice betraying cold or fear or both. "And it feels warmer."

There was no hum of machinery. No whisper of cloth or murmur of voices save their own. The place felt deserted, though Dale wasn't yet ready to trust his feelings.

She was right. His face was warmer than his back. He moved toward the heat, aware of Tansy close behind him, and stopped dead when he reached a man-high opening in the gem wall and smelled the warm, moist air coming from the natural antechamber.

An opening high above them let in the light, which filtered through a jutting purple stone to give the grayness a touch of lavender.

Tansy's gasp reverberated through his body, setting up greedy little thrills and warning bells. "Is that…?"

He nodded, though he wasn't sure anymore what he was agreeing to. "Yep. It's a hot spring."

Chapter Twelve

It shouldn't have been awkward for them to undress together. They'd done it a hundred times on assignments before they became lovers, and many more times since. But Tansy turned away from him now, and her fingers shook from more than cold as she tugged at her shirt and pants.

After an agonizing moment, he turned away. "I'm going to scout the rest of the cave and make sure there's really nobody here. I'll probably take a look outside, too."

"Be careful," she called, but was grateful when he was gone. Hot baths and Dale were a potent combination. She wasn't sure she'd be strong enough to resist, even though she'd come to grips with the fact that they would go their separate ways once they left Lobster Island.

If they left Lobster Island.

"No. I won't think like that," she said aloud, wincing when the strange crystal walls picked up her words and threw them back at her.

She listened for Dale, or for gunshots, but the doctor in her knew that Roberts would soon be irrelevant if she didn't bring her body temperature up. Though it was probably forty degrees outside, the wind and the rain made it feel far colder. She debated keeping on her panties and bra, then shrugged, wrung them out and added them to the line of clothing she'd spread on the gritty floor along one wall. Hopefully, the warm air and the slight breeze from the hurricane winds above would be enough to dry them.

When she dipped a toe into the oily-looking water that swirled in a rocky bowl near the far wall of the eerie cavern, she found the water blood-warm. Slipping in, she felt strange mineral salts tingling against her skin. With a sigh, she let her head fall back and felt the warmth caress her scalp. Warm. She was finally warm. She arched up and felt the heavy mineralized water sheet off her breasts.

"God." The single word in Dale's voice was less a curse than a prayer.

Tansy straightened in the chest-high water, aware that it all but glowed amethyst around her. Dale stood near the door with the shotgun in one hand and a knapsack in the other. His eyes were fixed on her.

"I found some food near the back of the main cave," he said thickly. "It's not much, but it's packaged, so it should be safe. I also found three unopened cases of saxitoxin from Beverly Labs. I think we can be safe in assuming he didn't poison the island."

The reminder of their peril should have been

enough to jerk her back to reality, but the purple light and the man standing at the water's edge wouldn't allow Tansy to climb back up out of the rabbit hole. Part of her wanted to stay down here forever.

"I, uh, found some string in a pile of equipment, and rigged a trip wire at the front. If anyone comes in, the noise will warn us." He took another step closer to the water, eyes dark in the strange half light of the storm that raged far away, outside the suddenly steamy cave.

"You've done your best, Dale. Now come and get warm. You must be freezing." She patted the water beside her and saw his eyes flash with the memories that crowded her head, as well.

There was no future for them, she knew, but what was the harm in one last moment in the present?

He dropped the knapsack near the water's edge and set the gun beside it. "We should probably take turns bathing. It'll be safer."

She lifted an eyebrow. "Roberts is gone, Dale. Even if he made it out of the river alive, there's no way Harriet is letting him—or one of his friends— back up here today." As if in confirmation, the hurricane winds blasted past the rocky opening high overhead, creating an eerie, moaning descant that raised the hairs on Tansy's body as she stood in the warm water. "We're safe enough for right now."

"That wasn't what I meant." His voice rasped on the words and Tansy realized what he'd meant by "safe."

She wouldn't be safe from him, or from the wild urges she'd seen reflected in his eyes after Roberts had gone downriver.

"Oh." Suddenly hotter than the surrounding steam, Tansy patted the water again and felt the ripples tingle at the tops of her breasts. "Then come into the water, Dale. Please."

She would give herself this one last, unwise interlude before she said goodbye.

She thought he muttered a curse, or maybe a prayer, then he was in the water with her, fully clothed, pressing her up against the smooth, warm amethyst that lined the hot spring. But instead of kissing her right away, and grinding at her with the abandon of her dreams, he caught her face between his hands. "Tans. I never meant to put you in danger. I want you to know how sorry I am."

A quick lump plugged her throat, hard and hot, and she smiled defiantly past it. "Hey," she said softly, "what happened to the guy whose first words to me were, 'Don't slow me down'?"

"He got to know you."

For a brief moment, she wondered what that might mean, then the wondering floated away on a purple beam of light as he kissed her, and the wind above gave an eerie, triple-noted moan.

Or maybe that was her.

On a sigh, she curled her arms around his neck, quivering slightly as the breeze chilled them in an instant. The roughness of his clothes against her naked skin was a tantalizing, impossible friction when she lifted her legs to wrap them around his waist.

They'd loved each other like this before. But the strange-colored darkness, the storm and the danger outside and her sure knowledge that this was the last time for them, lent a sharpness to her desire. She felt an edgy need to brand herself on his skin as he had tattooed himself on her heart.

So she broke the kiss to slide lower in the water and rake her teeth, hard, across the place where his neck and his shoulder joined.

He hissed sharply and jerked her up so they were eye to eye. Nose to nose. "Be sure, Tansy. You don't know me."

But she did. She knew the wildness that came from this island, and the honor that came from Dale himself. She also knew the barriers, and the things he was incapable of doing.

Like loving her.

"I'm sure," she said firmly. "I'm sure that I want this, just as I'm sure we'll say goodbye once we return to Boston."

When she said it like that, it seemed like making it back home was certain. The small lie felt good.

He frowned. "That's not what I meant."

She kissed the corners of his mouth where it turned down, and busied her fingers with his shirt. Her hands were trembling again, but not from the cold. Now they shook with want. With need.

With the power that flowed between them.

"No. But it's what you've always wanted." And she took his mouth and poured three long, lonely months into one kiss until they both trembled with it.

Then there was no more need for words, no place for them. They wrestled his sodden clothes off, tossing them in wet heaps beside the pool. Tansy tasted him, feasted on him, storing up the memories for the lonely times she knew would soon come. When his head snapped back with a groan, she fastened her teeth on his lower lip and slid down his shaft, feeling her hips crack against stone when he surged deep and hard and sure to touch her center.

Her heart.

She clenched around him and he cried out, surging against her again as a quick, sharp wave broke over them both, leaving them quivering with aftershocks and frustration.

Tansy almost cursed as remembered reality intruded. She'd wanted this last time to be tender. Perfect. Emotional. But it had just been about sex.

Then again, that had been their problem from the beginning.

Feeling tears burn behind her lids, she pushed against his chest.

"Not yet," he said quietly, pressing her back against the sloping wall of the hot spring. "Please, not yet."

Surprised, she let herself relax against him, aware of the pulsing place where they were still joined. Almost unwillingly, she curled her arms and legs around him, knowing the sense of security was a lie.

But who the hell cared? She buried her face against his neck and hung on tight, hoping he couldn't tell that her tears mingled with the warm water surrounding them.

His arms tightened around her and he sighed, a deep motion that was echoed where he still nestled within her.

"My mother would have liked you," he finally said. Tansy stilled. After a moment of silence, broken only by the sound of the wind above them and the gentle slap of water against semiprecious stone, he continued, "And my father, too."

Part of her didn't want to ask, knowing that it still wouldn't be enough. Her mother had been wrong. Knowledge wasn't power.

Love was.

But the pain in his voice called to the healer in her. She closed her eyes and felt the tears leak through. "What were they like?"

"Plain and honest. Poor but happy. Like the island," he said. And there was a touch of surprise in his voice when he added, "I wish I was more like them."

Not sure how to help, not sure she wanted to, Tansy turned into him and tried to heal his wounds with a kiss. Tried to heal her own, though she'd brought them on herself.

"Tans," he murmured, sliding against her and returning the caress of her tongue and lips. "Sweetheart."

She shut her heart to the endearment, to the false hope it brought, and shaped his face with her hands as she kissed him, trusting him not to let her sink beneath the warm water.

Wishing she could sink down and never come back up, breaking through back into reality.

The purple air spun out around them as he hardened within her once again. There was no frenzy to their coupling this time, though no less desire. A move. A splash. A sigh. Sound and texture became one as the sky darkened outside, dusk coming unnoticed amidst the storm.

After a time, they crawled up onto the ledge, laughing over their water-wrinkled skin and feeding each other bits of the packaged crackers Dale had found. They wrung out his clothes and left them beside hers to dry before returning to the smooth spot they'd discovered beside the hot spring, where soft, worn stone cushioned their bodies, and steam from the spring kept them warm.

And he talked. He told her about his Aunt Sue, and how Trask had fallen apart after her death. He told her about leaving the island and being afraid. And he told her about seeing himself as a fake, though in her mind there was no one at Boston General less false than Dale Metcalf. He made no apologies for his barriers, simply expected the rest of the world to live with them.

And now that the barriers were coming down?

"It's no good," she murmured, rolling away from him just after dawn, when even the hot spring seemed cooler. She shivered in the humid air and thought she felt her heart crack. She couldn't do this.

He followed her. "What's no good?" His voice was raspy with fatigue and stress. And maybe something else.

"You. Me. Us." She closed her eyes, though the tears leaked through. Then she stilled, and her wounded heart picked up its beat with a spurt of fear. "Wait. Listen."

Silence. Finally, he said, "I don't hear anything." But he caught her tension, rose and padded to where their clothes had almost dried.

"That's the point."

"Oh, hell." He tossed her clothes over and pulled on his own. "The storm's passed."

And as though called down by his words, sunlight speared through the opening high above their resting place. It refracted through the crystal spear and bathed the room in purple light. But the shimmering light didn't feel restful now. It felt wrong, as though the morning sun shouldn't be that color. As though the hot spring was stained, bruised.

Tansy shuddered and hurried to dress. "You think Roberts is working with someone here on the island, don't you? You think there'll be someone waiting for us."

"If we're lucky, there won't be." Dale hefted the empty shotgun. "Let's get out of here. If we work our way down the hill on the other side, we should be able to make it back to town in a few hours." Neither of them bothered to mention the possibility of booby traps. It was a given.

Roberts and his partner didn't want this cave found. Part of her could understand the greed. Even lit with the strange purple light, the hot spring room was incredible, flanked on both sides of its entrance by towering rock stalagmites that thrust up and met at—

Tansy paused and looked more carefully. "Dale. I think there's another opening."

He followed her gesture and his eyes narrowed. "You're right. I missed it last night with the flashlight." He stuck his head through the crude door and his shoulders stiffened. He jolted back with a curse.

"What?" She moved to touch his arm, but stopped herself. "Dale, what's wrong? What is it?"

"It's Roberts. He's dead."

"Oh, God." She pushed past Dale's restraining arm and ducked into the narrow granite fissure, stalling when she saw the developer's body crumpled in the corner. He was wearing navy trousers, a wrinkled white shirt and one loafer. His head lolled at an obscene angle and his skin seemed tinted a strange gray-purple in the gem-filtered light. "His neck's broken."

At her elbow, Dale nodded. "And he didn't walk up here. Not in loafers."

Tansy shuddered. "That wasn't him in the forest, was it?" The question was rhetorical. There was no way the man could have fallen in the river and wound up in the cave, dry. "It was never him."

"Or he was part of it," Dale countered, "and his partner got spooked when we stayed on the island. Roberts was in the motel the night before last…"

And while they'd been sleeping in Eddie's room, someone had killed him, maybe even in the room next door. Tansy's skin crawled at the thought, and at the knowledge that they were several hours away from civilization, maybe a day away from the promised mainland rescue.

"Come on. Let's get out of here." Dale didn't finish his thought, but there was no need. Hurricane Harriet had come and gone, leaving them vulnerable. The killer might even now be on his way back up the southern claw to finish what he'd started.

As one, they turned for the exit of the narrow fissure. And stopped. There, on a small folding card table, sat a portable satellite phone. A wire snaked up to a crack in the stone, likely leading to a discreet dish.

"Of course," Dale muttered. "He'd need a way to communicate with his partner." He glanced quickly at Tansy, his expression cool and closed. Hurt.

They knew of only one other satellite phone on the island.

"Call Cage," Tansy finally said, "and tell him to hurry with our reinforcements. I'll keep watch in the main cave."

She could see that Dale didn't like it, but there weren't many options left.

He finally nodded. "Okay. But take this." He handed her the shotgun. "It's empty, but it might work as a threat."

Tansy swallowed hard and took the heavy gun, hating the feel of the stock in her hands, and hating even more that it was empty. She looked up at Dale and their eyes caught and held. His were full of emotions she'd never seen there before, emotions she'd longed for, begged for. But she steeled herself against the pull. She'd been down that road before.

In the end, she looked away and said simply, "Hurry. I'd rather be in the woods than stuck here—" her eyes drifted to Roberts's corpse "—with him."

"Tans—" Dale reached for her and she stepped back. He let his hand fall. "Tans, when we're out of here...when we're back at Boston General...I think we should talk."

So he could break up with her all over again. Damn him.

Ignoring the thud of hurt she'd brought on herself, Tansy turned away. "There's no need to talk, Dale. We've said all there is to say. When we get home, I'll ask for my transfer. Don't worry, I won't bother you with my emotions anymore."

Dale cursed as she walked out of the small fissure and into the hot spring chamber. "That wasn't what I— Tansy!" When she didn't turn back, he cursed again. "Fine. We'll talk about this later." She was almost to the outer cave when his final words carried to her. "Be careful, damn it."

"You, too," she murmured as she retraced her steps out to the main cave. The smooth purple sand was scuffed where she and Dale had entered the cave the night before.

And where three other sets of tracks had followed.

"Dale! There's someone else—" She spun to run back for him and stopped dead in her tracks.

Hazel and Trask huddled, bound and gagged, near a crumbling rock slide at the back of the cave. Their captor stood not two paces away from Tansy.

She stared at the revolver in the murderer's hand and felt the shotgun slip from her fingers. Heard it clatter to the floor. "You!"

Churchill's tie was askew and there was a smear of mud on his pant leg. Aside from those small imperfections—and the gun—he could have been standing before a board of directors in any big city. He smiled slightly. "Yes, my dear. Me." The cultured tones were society-perfect, but the wild look in his brown eyes was anything but. He grabbed her arm and his soft-looking fingers bit deep. "Now. Let's go take care of some business, shall we?"

The last thing Tansy saw as he dragged her toward the hot spring was the anguish in Hazel's eyes and the dull resignation in Trask's.

They didn't think she was coming back. And at that moment, neither did she.

THE SECRETARY'S VOICE was slightly distorted by the satellite connection. "Boston General Hospital, please hold."

"No! Wait! Damn it!" Dale banged his fist on the

rock ledge beside the communications device. It was a stroke of luck that they'd found the phone, and a source of great concern.

Someone was bankrolling this illicit mining operation, probably the men who had hired Roberts to negotiate the purchase of the entire island. But who were they? How had they learned of the gems in the first place?

The answer pushed at him, demanding entrance through the closed wall of history, through the belief in the one man he'd trusted so many years ago. Churchill. He pushed the name away and concentrated on the feel of the phone in his hand, and the tension that hummed through him at the thought that Tansy was guarding the entrance to the cave with an empty shotgun.

The line remained stubbornly on hold, but unless he could get through to Cage, only Hazel and Trask would know where they were, and Dale wasn't certain they'd made it. The thought that his uncle and Hazel might be gone ached through his chest like a wound, but he couldn't dwell on that now. He had to focus on getting Tansy back to town safely.

Though he'd felt her pulling away more and more as the night wore on, uncomfortable with the man he truly was, in the darkest hours before the dawn, Dale had decided there was no way he was letting her go. He'd fight for her if he had to.

Then he would deal with the rest. Right now, she was his first priority. And if he had his way, she'd be his first priority for the rest of their lives.

If only he could make her believe that.

The phone clicked in his ear. "Head Administrator's office, one mom—"

"No!" Dale barked. "Janice, it's Dale Metcalf. Don't you dare put me on hold! I have to talk to Cage. Now. I'm in trouble."

Janice didn't respond. She rang him through.

"Metcalf. What's wrong?" Cage's voice boomed down the scratchy line, familiar and welcome, sharp with anxiety. "Why the hell haven't you contacted me before now? Is Tansy okay?"

Dale felt an unexpected surge of relief. He'd never consciously realized how much he depended on the HFH structure. But knowing it was there gave him the strength to fly out into the field, never knowing what to expect. He took a breath. "She's fine." He hoped. "I need the plane and the feds here as soon as you can arrange it. We're in trouble."

There was a confused silence, then Cage asked, "What plane? Feds? Dale, what the hell have you two gotten yourselves into?"

Oh, God. Dale's blood ran cold, then hot, as that nagging answer solidified to fact. Only one other person on the island had a satellite phone, and he'd called Cage for reinforcements.

At least he'd said he had.

"Metcalf? What's going on? Talk to me!"

Dale dropped the phone.

Tansy!

Chapter Thirteen

Churchill dragged Tansy into the hot spring chamber. She dug in her heels and felt them slide on stone when he yanked her arm and snarled, "Cut it out, you—"

"I wouldn't do that, Walter." Dale stepped out from behind a spear of purple and green. His eyes were cool and hard, emotionless and unsurprised. "Let her go."

But for once, Tansy could read the feelings beneath his mask—betrayal. Churchill. The one man he'd trusted. The man who'd saved him from Trask's drunken rages and helped him become a doctor.

His surrogate father. The man he'd tried to make himself into.

The man who'd killed his parents.

"I don't think so, Dale," Churchill replied, sounding unruffled, though his muscles were tense and his fingers trembled where they gripped her arm hard enough to bruise. "I need to talk to you, to make you understand." The gun barrel dug into the soft flesh beneath Tansy's jaw, and she bit back a whimper. "I figure as long as I have her, you're not going to do anything rash."

"Rash?" Dale's eyes snapped with temper. "You've got the gun, Churchill, which means I'm going to listen to you whether I want to or not. Let her go. She means nothing to me. We broke up months ago."

But Tansy could see the lie in his words.

Apparently Churchill couldn't. He grunted and dragged her back into the main cave, letting her fall near Hazel and Trask.

Dale followed, seeming calm. A subtle tightening around his mouth was his only reaction to finding the others bound and gagged. He glanced over at Churchill. "You wanted to talk? So talk."

He stepped toward the cave mouth, forcing Churchill to turn away from the others. Tansy righted herself and slid along the wall until she reached Hazel. Unfortunately, the madman caught her motion and turned fiery brown eyes on her.

"Where the hell do you think you're going? Stay the hell still!" He kicked her in the ribs, hard.

Black and purple pain exploded through Tansy. She gritted her teeth and rode it, glaring at Churchill through tearing eyes.

"You *bastard!*" Dale leapt forward and scooped the empty shotgun off the floor, ready to swing it, butt first, at Churchill's head.

"Stop!" Churchill barked. "You don't want to do that." He leveled the gun at Trask, then Hazel. Finally, Tansy. "Which one do you want to risk? All of them?" Dale subsided and the old man smiled his cultured, out-of-place smile. "Very good. Now, let's talk. I have a proposition for you."

He moved to the center of the sandy cave floor and gestured Dale back, farther from the others. As he stepped away, Dale locked eyes with Tansy, and the contact whispered through her like a caress.

I love you, his look seemed to say. *I won't let you down.*

And though it was probably a delusion brought on by at least two cracked ribs, Tansy let the emotion flow through her and return to him, hopeless though it was. *I love you, too.*

His eyes widened fractionally and she wondered whether he'd gotten her message, or whether it was all in her mind.

"What?" Churchill spun around and glared at Tansy, who curled up even tighter and clutched at her ribs.

When bone grated against bone, she didn't need to fake the raw hurt in her groan. God. Her vision grayed and she felt a gentle touch on her ankle. She focused on the feeling, and on Hazel's dear, scared eyes, until full consciousness returned.

"So what sort of a proposition do you have for me?" Dale asked, seeming interested in the answer, apparently willing to make a deal as he edged back towards the cave entrance, forcing Churchill to follow him. "And how much of the take from this place will I get?"

The old man chuckled. "That's my boy."

Ignoring the pain in her ribs and the fear in her heart, Tansy straightened as best she could, slid over beside Trask and got to work on the rope knotted around his wrists. Suddenly, from nowhere and everywhere came the memory of making love with Dale in the argent pool. Her fingers slipped, then steadied, as Dale led Churchill farther away, buying her time to free the others.

Partners to the end, she thought, and the warm glow of his trust worked its way through her, doing absolutely nothing to banish the dark danger around them.

"I'M NOT YOUR BOY," DALE replied, forcing his voice level when he wanted to rail at the man. "I loved my parents."

A spasm of grief passed across Churchill's face, the face Dale had so long remembered as the man who had saved him from life on Lobster Island, a fate he'd once considered far worse than death.

But were those his words, or Churchill's? It was hard to remember those hated, unhappy days after his parents died. He wasn't even sure whose idea it had been for him to leave.

"Yes. I was truly sorry for their loss, my boy." Churchill shook his head and tsked in sorrow. "But when your mother showed me the amethyst before she told anyone else about it, I knew it was a sign. I was meant to control this wealth." His grand gesture encompassed the whole glittering cave, and Dale's eyes locked on the gun.

Did he dare?

One part of his mind weighed the risk while the other part kept Churchill talking. Out of the corner of his eye, he saw Trask working on Hazel's bonds. Tansy was creeping across the cave, her attention divided between Churchill and something in the far, shadowed corner of the main cave.

Keep Walter occupied, her eyes seemed to say. *Keep him talking.*

He didn't know what she planned, but her actions lent desperation to his plan. He had to disarm Churchill before any of the others were hurt.

Dale wouldn't let anything happen to his family. Never again.

Luckily, Churchill didn't need any prompting, as though all these years he'd believed that Dale would thank him for his quick thinking. "—and when the four of us, me, your parents and your aunt, reached the river, I saw right away what had happened. The big storms had washed out part of the ledge, bringing the amethysts down. We climbed up to investigate the cave, and, *boom!*" He clapped his hands together and shrugged. "The cave-in was a sign, you see? A sign that I was meant to have the wealth all to myself."

A cave-in. Dale closed his eyes in quick pain. His parents had died in the cave, not at sea.

"I didn't kill them, boy." Churchill's voice was

quiet, and his eyes strayed toward the pile of worn rubble at the far end of the cave. "And I tried to make it up to you. I will, if you'll let me." He held out both hands, gun and all, and for a moment he looked like a lonely, old man.

But Dale's voice was harsh when he said, "And what about the others you've killed? In the pit traps, and with the fake outbreak?"

Keep him talking, Tansy mouthed from twenty feet behind Churchill as she worked her way from the back of the cave on silent feet, favoring her side only slightly. Glass flashed in her palm.

"The others?" Churchill shrugged, and his eyes shifted from lonely to not-quite-right. "What did they matter? The cave is mine. It's up to me to protect it. These Yankees," he sneered and spat, "don't know a good offer when they hear one. If they'd sold fifteen years ago when I first tried to buy them out, they'd all have been safe. It was their fault, really, that I had to buy the lobster fleet and live here. I had to protect the cave."

Tansy was mere steps away from Churchill, her eyes fixed on the soft place where the old man's flabby neck joined his weak shoulder.

"So you've starved the islanders, keeping them poor and waiting for them to sell." Dale tried to push admiration into his voice, but feared it was a failure.

Churchill sickened him. Worse, his own snobbery and desire to see himself as better than the islanders sickened him.

He wasn't better than Lobster Island. He wasn't good enough for it.

Churchill must have sensed his hesitation. The old man's face twisted and he took a step nearer Dale, away from Tansy. "You understand, don't you, boy? You know why I've done it. All this—" He waved around the cave, indicating the glorious streams of color that were waking up now that the sun was shining. A beam shot through an opening high above the cave and light refracted off spears of pure color. Dale saw himself reflected off a prism across the cave.

And Churchill saw Tansy directly behind him with an ampoule of saxitoxin in her hand.

"No!" he yelled, throwing up his arm to ward off the blow.

Dale flung himself across the remaining feet and tackled Churchill at the waist, bringing him down, hard. They rolled together almost to the edge of the cliff, and the gun went off, roaring like thunder in the echoing cave, again and again as Churchill fired randomly and Tansy dove for cover.

The rock, Dale. Your lucky rock. His mother's voice seemed to echo in his head, or maybe from the back of the cave, where rain had eaten away at the rubble. Dale grabbed the broken stone in his pocket and brought it up between them when Churchill reversed the roll and sent them back into the cave.

Pain sliced through Dale's hand, then was gone. Churchill stiffened with a wet croak. His hands scrabbled feebly at Dale's shirt, then at his own. They came away wet with blood. Then slowly, slowly they relaxed and fell by the old man's sides. His eyes glazed over, and a final puff of air passed between his lips, carrying one last word.

"Son…"

After a long, disbelieving moment, Dale rolled away, leaving the glittering crystal shard embedded in Churchill's chest. He looked at his hand, where the lucky stone had cut his palm, then across the cave to Tansy. His Tansy. "Are you okay?"

With a choked sob, she threw herself across the space between them. "I thought he was going to…I thought you…"

Dale caught her close, though he tried to be careful of her ribs, where Churchill had kicked her. For that, Dale wished he could kill the evil old bastard all over again. "I know. I thought so, too." He buried his face in her hair and felt all of the emotions he'd so often kept deep down inside bubble up to the surface. "I'm so damned sorry, Tans."

She pulled away slightly, wincing at the motion. But her eyes were intent. Fierce. "If you apologize once more for bringing me here, I'm going to shoot you myself. I—"

"Not for bringing you here," he interrupted, feeling the boiling emotions smooth over into one glowing, golden conviction. "I'm sorry I never told you that I—"

"Trask?" Hazel's voice, sharp and worried,

broke into the moment. "Trask, what's wrong? Are you hurt?"

Suddenly fearing that one of the stray bullets had winged his uncle, Dale levered himself and Tansy to their feet, though he kept one arm wrapped around her, needing the contact.

Needing to know she was still there, because he had no intentions of ever letting her go. Almost unconsciously, his free hand dipped into his pocket, where his mother's engagement ring now rested alone.

Then he saw his uncle's face, and everything inside him went cold. Oh, God. The graves.

Trask's eyes were glued to the rubble at the far end of the cave, which looked to have been pierced by a recent flood runoff. A beam of sunlight caromed into the small space, and something glinted near the cave-in. Something golden. With a low moan, Trask pulled free from Hazel and crossed to the spot. He knelt down by the rubble and bowed his head over what might have been a wedding ring.

With a low murmur of pain, Tansy pulled away from Dale and crossed the open mouth of the cave, intent on helping the grieving man. The sun glowed through the entrance, silhouetting her for a moment that seemed frozen in time as Dale heard a muffled, incongruous *pop* from outside.

Tansy stiffened, and fell without a sound.

"Tansy!" Dale felt his heart explode into a million terrified pieces. He bolted the few steps that separated them, but was kept on his feet by the dark, lean silhouette that appeared in the cave mouth. The dark green raincoat was familiar.

The woman wearing it, less so.

"Step back over by your uncle, please, Mr. Metcalf." Frankie waved her silenced weapon over to the side, then returned it to level between his eyes. "I'm afraid I can't let any of you leave this cave."

Dale raised his hands and stepped back, cursing himself for having forgotten about Churchill's bodyguard. In that instant, as he listened to Tansy's shallow, quick breaths tailing off with a bubble at the end, Dale remembered Frankie tossing Trask's drunken dead weight over her shoulder and carrying him home. Idiot. He'd never stopped to think that Churchill couldn't have carried Roberts up the hill alone. Frankie had been in on it from the beginning.

Or if not from the beginning, for long enough.

Dale was aware of Trask at his back, and Hazel. He was aware of the woman he loved, bleeding into the purple sand of the cave floor.

And over it all, he was aware of a growing red haze, anger at the people and the greed that had changed his life once before and wanted to ruin him again.

Then Frankie stood over Tansy's limp body and leveled her weapon.

And Dale broke.

"Damn it, no!" he yelled. He dove for Churchill's corpse and scooped up the gun the old man had dropped in his death spasms, hoping against hope the bullets weren't spent. Not caring whether Frankie shot him, caring only to protect the woman he'd sworn to save, Dale squeezed the trigger over and over again.

There were two shots, then a volley of clicks as the hammer fell on empty chambers.

Blood sprayed from Frankie's thigh, and she staggered backward, onto the smooth sand at the cave's mouth. She leveled her weapon at Dale and fired. Her leg buckled, and a scream of anguish stretched her mouth as she overbalanced and toppled backward.

Out of the cave and down the almost-sheer rock face.

Her scream ended with a horrible gurgle, and the occupants of the cave stayed frozen for an endless moment. Then Hazel scrambled to Tansy's side, took one look at her and barked, "Come on, Dale. Help me over here. I need you. Tansy needs you."

"God. Oh, God." But for once it wasn't a curse. It was a prayer. Dale dropped to his knees beside her and slid her limp form onto his lap. He was careful of the ribs that grated as he moved her, and lifted her slightly so her wounded shoulder was above the level of her heart. "Through and through," he muttered when Hazel joined him. "Looks clean."

It would be a simple fix, they both knew, with a few basic supplies. But there were no basic supplies in Churchill's cave, and the blood was welling too fast, too thick to be ignored.

"We have to get her to the motel," Hazel said quietly, a tremble in her voice betraying the stress of the last half day. "If we don't…"

"We will," Dale snapped. "Nothing's going to happen to her." He raised his voice, hating the sharp echoes of the cave, hating everything about it. "Trask, get over here. We need to carry Tansy down."

The older man was up to his knees in rubble, pushing rocks aside with his bare hands. "In a minute. I've almost reached her."

The rawness in his voice was no more wrenching than the look of defeat on Hazel's face, but Dale would hurt for them later. Tansy was his priority right now.

She always had been. He just hadn't wanted to admit it.

"No," he said quietly, but there was an underlying power that gave his uncle pause. "I need you now."

Trask stopped digging, then sighed, nodded and stood. "You're right. I'm sorry." And it seemed that he included Hazel in the apology.

They snapped curved branches from the trees outside and bound them together with Churchill's tie and strips torn from his fine linen shirt. Dale saw the monograms at the collar and cuff, and winced, then put the old man out of his mind as they carried Tansy down the cliff and across the storm-swollen river. She surfaced to shallow consciousness once or twice during the four-hour trek back down to the beach.

Each time her eyelids fluttered, Dale gripped her hand and leaned close to her ear to whisper. "I love you. Do you hear me? I love you. Stay with me. You can do it. Hang tough. *I love you.*"

But he was never sure that she heard the words. The blood kept seeping through the crude pressure bandages, and as they neared the end of their trek, her color faded to pale, then near-white.

Then they reached the beach, and were greeted by chaos.

"What the hell happened?" Cage snapped, charging halfway up the path to meet them. "You said she was fine."

"She was," Dale answered faintly, trying to decide if the HFH helicopter on the beach was an exhausted delusion or not.

"Get her in the chopper. There are first aid-kits on board. We can have her at Boston General by nightfall."

Without thinking, Dale shook his head. "No. She stays here." He turned back to the makeshift litter, which they'd placed across the back seat of Trask's waterlogged jeep, and found Tansy conscious. Her eyes were blurred with pain, but her lips twisted in a faint smile.

"I thought you didn't want me here." Her words were faint but clear.

"I didn't," he replied automatically, then stopped and closed his eyes. "I didn't," he repeated, "but I do now." He opened his eyes and glanced from Hazel to Trask, then out to the water, where the curve of the lobster's tail could be seen across the misty whitecaps. He took a deep breath and gathered all the courage he could never seem to find before.

"I don't have much to offer you," he said with a small smile, "besides a burned down house and a dead tree." Then he sobered. "And myself." He took her hand and winced at the stain of fresh blood on the pressure bandage. "Never mind. We can do this later, after you've been seen to." He tried to step away and wave the others in to apply their first aid.

But she wouldn't let go of his hand. "No way, Metcalf." Her voice was strong, her eyes brighter than they'd been moments before. "Keep going."

Dale was suddenly aware of the crowd that had gathered around the jeep. Mickey was there with his family—they must have led the HFH helicopter to the beach. A number of other islanders had followed, and they stood on the shifting sands amid the HFH doctors Cage had brought with him. And almost every one of the islanders was related to Dale in one way or another.

They were his family.

And at that realization, it was as though the steel band that had been wrapped around Dale's heart for so many years finally let go, carrying a gush of emotions with it. He bowed his head and, incredibly, felt a huge grin split his face.

I love you, whispered a voice in his heart. Then, in case she hadn't heard the words, Dale lifted his eyes to hers and said, "I love you."

A single tear slid down her cheek. "And what else?"

What else. The message was clear. Tansy wasn't going to accept half measures from him anymore. Well, that was fine. He wasn't giving them anymore. He reached into his pocket and pulled out his mother's ring, held it up to the light.

A second tear glittered down to join the first.

"I love you," he repeated, "and I want to marry you. I want to rebuild my parents' house with you, and I want us to help bring Lobster Island back to life. A new clinic. A new school. Whatever it takes."

Without a word, she held up a trembling left hand. Dale slid the ring onto her third finger, where it fit snugly, as though it never intended to let go.

Well, that was fine because neither did he.

"Is that a yes?" he asked, knowing from the love shining in her eyes that it was, but needing to hear the words as much as he needed to say them.

She nodded and gave him a watery smile. "That's a yes."

The words were barely out of her mouth before Cage's paramedics descended upon the jeep, packing and stabilizing her wound and preparing her for transport—not to Boston General, but to Hazel's motel clinic.

When they arrived at the clinic, Hazel stood aside with Trask and didn't join the rush to treat Tansy. Dale paused, and Tansy held up a hand to stop them from carrying her inside the room where they'd saved Eddie's life.

"What's wrong?" Dale finally asked.

"I'm going with Trask," Hazel answered firmly. "We're going to do some digging." Her eyes were bright with unshed tears, but determined.

"No," Trask demurred. "We're going home."

When Hazel turned to him, he grinned crookedly. "You and me, we're going to have ourselves a yard sale. A really big one." His grin faded and his eyes found Tansy and Dale. "When Tansy's feeling better, we'll all go up the mountain and dig. It should be a family affair."

And Dale heard his mother's voice whisper in his heart.

Family.

He lifted Tansy's hand to his lips and pressed a kiss to the diamond-and-ruby ring. Then he followed her into the shabby motel room.

It was time for people to start living on Lobster Island. Again.

* * * * *

Coming in March 2005 from
Harlequin Intrigue, watch for
Jessica Andersen's breathtaking new medical
mystery! Danger lurks in the corridors of
Boston General Hospital—and it's up to two
lovelorn docs to unravel the clues.
Don't miss a moment of the thrills and chills
in COVERT M.D.